INTO THE DORKNESS

INTO THE DORKNESS

BY THE AUTHOR OF *THE ZOMBIE CHASERS*
JOHN KLOEPFER

ILLUSTRATED BY
NICK EDWARDS

HARPER
An Imprint of HarperCollinsPublishers

Galaxy's Most Wanted #2: Into the Dorkness

Library of Congress Cataloging-in-Publication Data
Kloepfer, John, author.
Into the dorkness / by John Kloepfer ; illustrated by Nick
Edwards. — First edition.
        pages   cm. — (Galaxy's most wanted ; #2)
Summary: Kevin and his science camp buddies, the
Extraordinary Terrestrials, defeated the alien Mim and sent him
back to prison—but now a group of his friends have shown up
in spaceships, bent on revenge, and it is up to the Extraordinary
Terrestrials to find a way to defeat the invaders.
ISBN 978-0-06-223109-3
1. Human-alien encounters—Juvenile fiction. 2. Extraterrestrial
beings—Juvenile fiction. 3. Science camps—Juvenile fiction.
[1. Extraterrestrial beings—Fiction. 2. Camps—Fiction. 3. Science
fiction. 4. Humorous stories. 5. Youth's art.] I. Edwards, Nick, 1990–
illustrator. II. Title.
PZ7.K6845In 2015   2014030715
[Fic] 813.6—dc23   CIP
                                                          AC

Typography by Ray Shappell
15 16 17 18 19 OPM   10 9 8 7 6 5 4 3 2 1
❖
First paperback edition, 2015

To Jordan, a good man and a better friend —J. K.

For Rosie —N. E.

The sky over Northwest Horizons Science Camp flashed and blinked with the lights from four massive UFOs hovering overhead. Standing next to the planetarium, Kevin Brewer and his friends stared slack-jawed at the extraterrestrial invasion swirling above them.

"What the heck is going on?" Kevin turned to face his friends Warner, Tara, and TJ as if any of them would have an answer. None of them did.

"I don't know," Tara said. "But I don't think we should stick around to find out."

Kevin glanced down at their miniaturized alien buddy, a cyborg space cop named Klyk, who Kevin had mistakenly blasted with a shrink ray the night before. Their alien friend ignored Kevin, unable to tear his eyes away from the UFOs headed their way.

Looking at their broken galactascope, Kevin couldn't believe how much trouble their science camp invention had caused. He and his team—the Extraordinary Terrestrials—had built the galactascope by following a diagram in one of Warner's sci-fi comic books. They had no idea the interstellar text messenger would actually work. Over the course of a few days, they had summoned the galaxy's most wanted alien, a purple furry creature named Mim with an appetite for destruction, fought off a giant arachnopod—a humongous half octopus, half tarantula—and saved the world from annihilation.

But right after sending Mim back to space prison, they discovered the purple planet-eater had managed to call his fellow space thugs for backup. Now Mim's alien associates had arrived on Earth, and Kevin didn't have the slightest clue about what to do next.

About a hundred yards away from Kevin and his friends, the rest of the Northwest Horizons campers were huddled together outside the mess hall. A prolonged hush fell over the adolescent mob as they all took in the sight of the alien spaceships roiling overhead.

The otherworldly fleet spread out high above the treetops to the four corners of the science camp. With a mechanical crank, the starships opened their doors, and each alien vessel then released half a dozen much smaller alien space cruisers.

A moment later, the clouds began to churn violently as a huge alien mother ship emerged from the atmosphere. The immense spacecraft blotted out the sun and cast a shadow over the camp below.

"Whoa," said Warner, his eyes lighting up with fear and excitement at the sight of the extraterrestrial invasion.

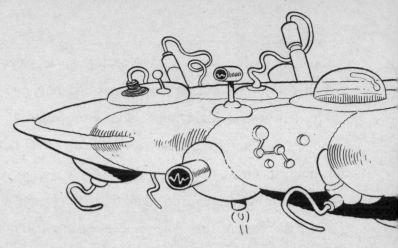

A hair-raising shriek pierced the awestruck silence. Kevin whipped his head around and gazed across the grounds of the science camp. Over by the dining hall, the throng of campers had erupted into a frenzy.

Kevin could hear Head Counselor Dimpus yelling instructions to his staff, trying to maintain control of his campers. "Start up the vans! Everybody stick together! Single-file lines!"

Dimpus then turned toward the planetarium and hollered at the Extraordinary Terrestrials. "Kevin! Warner! TJ! Tara! Get back here!"

But Kevin didn't twitch a muscle, frozen next to his dumbfounded friends. A huge loading hatch had

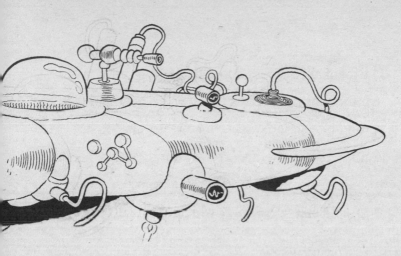

just started to open underneath the gargantuan alien mother ship.

"There's something coming out. . . ." TJ squinted through his thick-lensed glasses and tilted his head back. A few seconds later, a shimmering metallic sphere floated out of the hatch.

"What is that thing?" Tara asked.

Klyk gasped at the sight of the hovering metal sphere. "That thing is a freeze-ray bomb," he said. "And it means we need to run!"

"Wait," said Tara. "We have to warn the others!"

The sphere flew smoothly over the center of camp and stopped in midair directly above the hubbub of scrambling campers and counselors.

The giant alien sphere glowed a fluorescent orange.

"No time for that!" Klyk's tiny voice bellowed. The kids sprang into action, racing for the woods. "Run!"

Behind them, the freeze-ray bomb unleashed a bright bluish-white beam of plasma that spiraled straight to the ground like a tornado whirling down from the clouds.

Kevin scooped Klyk off the ground and put him on his shoulder.

"Pick it up, slowpoke!" Klyk shouted in Kevin's ear as they booked toward the Oregon pine forest. He hung on to Kevin's backpack strap as if he were riding a racehorse.

Kevin looked over his shoulder and back at the camp behind him.

VYRGHZ! The freeze-ray bomb let off a strange electrostatic noise as it detonated. A shock wave rippled out from the spot where the plasma beam struck the earth. The ground rumbled in response. The campers and counselors all halted in frozen poses of suspended animation as the freeze-ray bomb blast reverberated underfoot. It looked like someone hit the pause button on a raucous game of tag or capture the flag.

"Don't look back, Kevin!" Klyk shouted. "You're going to get us both zapped!"

Kevin's chest burned as he ran into the thicket of trees. But there was no time to catch his breath—and anyway, if he had, it would have been his last. He could feel the blue-white glow blazing hot on his trail as the pulse rushed up behind him.

Tara, Warner, TJ, and Kevin shuffle-stepped between a pair of pine trees and kept running headlong

into the forest. A frantic squirrel skittered down the tree beside Kevin. The blast radius of the freeze-ray bomb struck the base of the tree, and the squirrel paused mid-stride halfway up the trunk.

"Oh no!" Kevin gasped, huffing and puffing.

"Faster, Kevin, faster!" Klyk shouted.

Kevin pumped his arms and flung his feet forward, running with every ounce of energy he possessed. Ahead of them, Tara and Warner raced out of the woods and bolted across the soccer field that belonged to the all-girls soccer camp on the other side of the lake. Kevin looked to his right. He and TJ were neck and neck. The two slowpokes kept on chugging, trying to outrun the blue-white blast wave.

"Come on, Teej!" Kevin shouted, wheezing as the two of them raced out of the fast-freezing forest and high-stepped onto the soccer field.

"Oooph!" TJ grunted

loudly, and Kevin heard a thud.

Kevin swiveled his head to the side and out of the corner of his eye saw TJ stumble on a bump in the grassy turf. TJ tripped, flailing his arms. The freeze-ray bomb surged like a tide chasing up the backs of his legs.

Kevin thrust out his hand and grabbed TJ by the wrist. He planted his foot and heaved TJ ahead of the oncoming pulse.

TJ stumbled for a moment, then regained his balance and kept running. Kevin wasn't so lucky. He could feel the electromagnetic chill nip at his heels as he tripped and plunged face-first into the ground. *"OOMPH!"*

Klyk flew off Kevin's backpack and hit the turf, landing on both feet with perfect balance. The little alien bounded away from the freeze-ray swath gaining on them. Kevin tried to scramble to his feet, but he didn't have time to stand up. The freeze-ray bomb was moving too fast. As the bomb's pulse rippled toward his feet, Kevin sucked in one last breath and squeezed his eyes shut, ready to be frozen.

A few seconds passed and Kevin opened his eyes

gingerly. He wiggled his fingers and toes—everything still worked. The circumference of the blast wave had stopped just shy of his sneaker, leaving him about a millimeter out of range.

Kevin breathed a sigh of relief and tapped the stiff blades of grass with the tips of his cross-trainers.

"One of these days," he said to himself, and then collapsed back onto a bed of unfrozen green grass. "I'm going to have to get in better shape."

Lying on his back, Kevin thanked his lucky stars—Betelgeuse, Castor, Pollux, and Polaris. He sucked in a puff from his inhaler as Klyk and TJ raced to his side. Kevin turned his head to look at the miniaturized alien standing in front of his face. "We made it," he said.

"Barely," said Klyk, glancing at the borderline of rigid grass marking the outer reaches of the freeze-ray bomb blast. "You're one lucky earthling."

"Thanks for saving me, Kev," TJ said. He reached out his hand and lifted Kevin to his feet.

"No sweat, man," Kevin said, a drop of perspiration trickling down his face. "We all gotta stick together, right?"

11

He brushed himself off and caught his breath. Tara and Warner jogged back to the group and stopped in front of their team captain.

"Are you all right, Kevin?" Tara asked.

"Yup." Kevin bent his elbow and twisted at the waist. "Everything seems to be working okay."

"Good," she said. "Now can we get out of here, please?"

"The field house for the soccer camp's not too far away," Warner said, pointing toward another stretch of pinewoods on the other side of the field. "We can't just stay out in the open like this. We need to get away from those alien freaks before they catch up with us!"

"Wait," Klyk said. "We have to go back."

"What?" Tara asked. "Why?"

"For starters, we have no clue who we're dealing with," Klyk said. "And I can guarantee you they didn't come here to take over just your little science camp. If they were working with Mim, then they're not going to stop until they have control of the entire planet!"

Klyk was right. Whoever these aliens were, they

didn't seem to be fooling around. This alien invasion was the kids' mess and they had to clean it up. After all, they had taken down the galaxy's most wanted alien earlier that morning and now they were about to face off against his angry allies. That didn't make Kevin feel any more excited to go back after them. But they didn't have any other options. Whether they liked it or not, the choice had been made for them the moment they decided to try to contact alien life.

"You want us to go back and spy on those freeze-ray-bomb-toting alien maniacs?" Warner said. "Are you out of your mind?"

"I don't think so," Klyk said. "But I'll have to check the updates on my neuro-chip. There's no time for

that right now, though." The mini alien cyborg started to walk back toward the frozen forest.

"There's no way I'm going back there," Tara said.

"Me neither," Warner said.

"Suit yourselves," Klyk said. "But I'm getting to the bottom of this with you guys or without."

Kevin stepped across the line from the lush green grass to the blue-tinted blades where the freeze-ray blast had petered out.

"Dude, what are you doing?" Warner asked.

"I'm going with him," Kevin said. "It's our fault Mim came here in the first place. And now it's our

responsibility to take down these alien jerkfaces who are trying to mess up our summer!"

Kevin turned away from his friends to catch up with Klyk.

"What are you gonna do?" TJ looked at Tara and Warner. "When he's right, he's right," he said, and followed quickly after Kevin.

Warner groaned and glanced at Tara, who shrugged at him and hurried after TJ. Warner shook his head in disapproval and then broke into a jog to catch up with his friends.

The Extraordinary Terrestrials moved back toward

the tree line of the frozen pinewoods. The dirt felt hard as cement under their feet from the effects of the freeze-ray bomb.

Kevin waved to his friends, gesturing for them to follow him. They quickly fell in line and pushed deeper through the forest single file, crouching low to the ground. They strayed off the trail slightly, using the stiff frozen leafy bracken for cover.

"Come on, you guys," Kevin said. "I have an idea. If we keep heading along the path, it will lead us right to the robotics trailer on the other side of camp."

"So," Warner whispered behind Kevin. "What's the plan, man?"

"We're going to use the drone car from the robotics lab to spy on the aliens," Kevin said.

"But we never finished it," said Warner. "Remember? The receiver was broken."

"Yeah, I know, dude," Kevin said. "I was there. But if we put our heads together, I bet we can get it to work."

"Great idea, Kev!" said TJ. "This is gonna be sweet!"

"Yeah, except for the whole part about spying on a

bunch of psychotic aliens," Tara said, rolling her eyes. "Oh wait, that's the entire reason we're doing this."

"Tara," said Klyk earnestly. "If we don't find out what we're up against, whatever it may be, we'll be powerless to stop it."

Klyk climbed up Kevin's back and perched on his shoulder like a pet parrot. Staying low to the ground, Kevin crept back up to the walking path weaving through the woods.

"Hup . . ." Tara gasped, squinting through the foliage. "Kevin, wait! Don't . . ."

But it was too late.

About twenty yards off, a tall, lean figure lurked beyond the pines. The alien had the shape of a human-sized lizard. Some kind of alien weapon was slung over its shoulder.

Kevin froze in place while Klyk unzipped the backpack and dove into the pocket. Tara, Warner, and TJ all disappeared out of sight behind three different tree trunks.

Kevin stared straight ahead, stiff as a statue, as the alien strode toward him. Kevin's lungs tightened as he held his breath. The six-foot-six reptilian strolled silently down the path. The alien henchman stopped in its tracks and paused, flicking its gaze toward Kevin. Its head slinked to the side like a serpent gauging its prey before a strike.

Kevin held still, trying desperately not to shake or breathe or blink. He let his eyes go blank, avoiding eye contact. He had to look just as frozen as the camp around him.

The man-sized lizard alien took a few steps forward and stopped directly in front of Kevin. Its nostrils flared as it sized up Kevin's motionless form.

The reptilian grunted, and two puffs of hot breath

shot out of its nostrils. The stinking air hit Kevin's face and stung his eyes, making them water.

The immense alien reptile gave Kevin one more glance before continuing on with its patrol through the forest.

"What the heck was that thing?" Kevin whispered once the alien was out of earshot.

"That, my friend, was a Kamilion," Klyk said. "Part of a warrior race of reptilians with skin that can blend in with any background. I'm surprised there was only one of them—they usually travel in packs."

"You mean there could be more of those things?"

"There usually are," Klyk whispered in Kevin's ear. "But we're in the clear now. Let's keep moving. Before it's too late."

Kevin stopped at the brink of the forest and peered out past the lab trailers, scanning the campgrounds. In the distance, the campers and counselors looked like an outdoor gallery of wax figures trapped in awkward poses of shock, fear, and panic.

The lab trailer was only a short dash away. Kevin and the others had to be quick. At any second they could be spotted by one of the Kamilions.

"Okay, let's go!" Kevin ordered in a firm whisper. The five of them took off in a full sprint and skidded to a halt behind the mess hall, which was still covered in arachnopod silk.

Kevin touched the silk and remembered earlier

in the day when Mim's pet arachnopod—a half tarantula, half octopus named Poobah—had swallowed their shrink ray. They had reversed the shrink ray so it would actually enlarge anyone it zapped, in the hope that they could return Klyk back to his regular size. But when Poobah swallowed the alien technology, he suddenly grew to five times his normal size and began wreaking havoc on the camp. Kevin and his friends eventually defeated the gigantic alien beast—and retrieved their shrink ray—but not before it had cocooned everyone inside the mess hall.

It was only a few hours ago that they were fighting off Poobah, but it seemed like an eternity had passed. Events were occurring so quickly it felt as though time had become compressed, as though the seconds were ticking off the clock at the speed of light.

They had everything to lose and no time to spare.

Quietly they snuck past the extraterrestrial cocoon around the mess hall and hustled behind the trailers until they reached the entrance to the robotics lab. With Klyk on his shoulder, Kevin opened the door to the trailer and hurried in, followed by his three friends.

"Wait a sec," TJ said as he swung the door shut behind them. "Why isn't all this stuff freeze-rayed, too?"

"The freeze-ray bomb is unique because it only affects certain kinds of matter," Klyk explained. "People, animals, plant life, but not man-made objects like a regular freeze-ray would."

Kevin surveyed the room for the remote-controlled drone car they had begun a few weeks earlier at camp. "Perfect," he said, spotting it on a shelf across the lab. "It's right where we left it."

The five of them gathered around the storage rack. Their unfinished drone car was made from a regular remote-controlled truck that could be bought at any toy store. They had fashioned it with a microphone and wireless camera feed that in theory would transmit sound and video back to a monitor located in the lab. But they could never get a signal to transmit.

"Come on, let's take a look at this thing." Kevin lifted it off the shelf and carried it to the video monitor sitting on the worktable.

Warner, Tara, and TJ gathered around their project. TJ touched his forehead to Tara's temple and held it there.

"Umm, what are you doing?" she asked.

"I thought we were going to put our heads together?" TJ said. "Kidding!"

"Ba-dum ching!" Warner played an imaginary drumbeat for the punch line.

"TJ, now's not the time for practicing your

stand-up routine," Kevin said, gesturing back to the task at hand.

Tara made sure the camera was mounted properly. TJ tested the sound levels on the microphone. Then they turned on the motor of the toy car to make sure the mufflers were still working. They had silenced the noisy clattering whir of the battery-operated engine, coating it with memory foam. Now the drone car barely made a sound. Warner flicked the power switch for the transmitter while Kevin checked the wireless video receiver. Something was still wrong. The receiver wouldn't turn on.

"I told you that thing is busted," Warner said.

"Did you switch out the batteries?" Kevin asked.

"Yeah, I checked them twice," Warner said.

Kevin opened the battery pack and inspected the double As. He looked up and glared at his friend.

"Why are you looking at me like that?" Warner said. "I put in brand-new batteries last week, I swear!"

"Yes, you did." Kevin nodded. "But how do you expect the batteries to work if they're going in the wrong direction?" Kevin flipped the batteries around and popped the case back into place.

"Oops . . . ," Warner mumbled.

"Tsk-tsk." TJ made a cross with his index fingers and rubbed them at Warner. "What kind of science camper are you?"

"The cool kind," Warner protested. TJ just shrugged.

"Being a big ole dummy isn't cool, Warner," Tara added.

Kevin sat down at the video monitor with the homemade drone car. A few clicks later and the remote surveillance vehicle was up and running. Tara picked up the toy car and aimed the camera lens in front of her face like she was taking a selfie. Tara pouted her lips and batted her eyelashes, making a glamorous face like a supermodel.

They could see the video feed transmitting from the wireless camera to the computer monitor.

"Very nice, Tara—the camera loves you," Kevin said matter-of-factly. "Now it's time to send this bad boy out."

Tara took the truck to the open lab door and set it just outside on the freeze-ray-stiffened grass.

Warner used the remote control to steer it toward the center of camp.

"Warner, slow down!" Kevin said as they watched the monitor. "You're getting too close. They're gonna spot us!"

"Chill out, man," Warner snapped back. "I'm trying to get within audio range. Trust me, I know what I'm doing."

"Yeah, but—"

"Whoa!" TJ and Tara said, jinxing each other.

On the video monitor, they could see two alien ringleaders standing in the middle of their legion of reptilian henchmen at the center of the camp.

The larger of the two was long and lean, standing nearly seven feet tall. Its skin had a translucent sheen, so that its internal organs were nearly visible. Its slug-like face split off into two lobes, each housing one of its eye sockets. Its nose was nothing but two nostrils situated above a mouth with scaly lips that wrapped 180 degrees around its face.

The smaller alien wasn't much of anything at all, just a brain sheltered in a glass case. Its body was purely robotic, with four bionic legs and two protracting metallic arms. A hologram of a semi-human-looking face was projected on the curved surface of the glass case.

"Who are those dudes?" Tara asked.

"More like what are those dudes?" said Warner.

"Zouric and Nuzz." Klyk gulped. Even the tough-guy alien bounty hunter had a note of worry in his voice. "Zouric is a Gastropod," their little alien friend told them.

"You mean like a giant slug worm?" TJ asked.

"Basically," Klyk said; then continued, "Nuzz used to be a different type of Gastropod, but more human-like. He was killed in the Quasar Wars of 1011011001, but somehow they salvaged his brain and preserved his consciousness in that machine he walks around in." Klyk paused for a beat and shook his head. "These guys have been bad since before bad existed. Take a look."

Kevin, Warner, Tara, and TJ huddled around the mini alien cyborg as he pulled out his 3D holographic dossier. Klyk filled them in on the second and third most wanted criminals in the known universe.

"You ever run into them before?" Warner asked.

"Never face-to-face," the mini cyborg space cop said. "But my old partner squared off against the Gastropods during the

Quasar Wars. Not a good time for the galaxy. . . . Clurg—that was my partner's name— and Zouric were fighting on opposite sides. He told me that Zouric was one of the Gastropods' finest warriors."

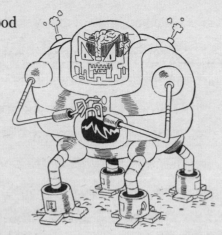

The kids looked back to the screen showing two of the galaxy's most wanted aliens in real time.

Zouric, the lanky seven-foot slug man, and Nuzz, the brain bot, strolled through the freeze-rayed camp with their army of Kamilions following behind them. They strode past the fallen arachnopod Poobah. After accidentally supersizing the alien creature, Kevin and the gang had finally taken it down by pelting the thing with tennis balls covered in Mim's fur, causing an allergic reaction in the mondo beast. Poobah was now lying on its side, frozen in a slumped heap of tentacles and hairy spider legs. Kevin wasn't even sure if the poor thing was still alive.

Zouric and Nuzz moved past the massive arachno-pod and strolled into the field of human statues.

Warner adjusted the camera angle on the drone car to follow them and zoomed in.

The two aliens spoke in some extraterrestrial language indecipherable to Kevin and his friends.

"What are they saying?" Tara asked Klyk.

"Just give me a minute," Klyk said, listening to the conversation intently over the video feed. Then he began to translate:

Zouric: Where's Mim?

Nuzz (angrily): He said the planet would be ready by now!

Zouric: Something must have gone wrong.

Nuzz: Of course something went wrong, you imbecile! There are still people on this planet.

Zouric: It's not my fault. I told you we shouldn't trust that little ball of fur.

Nuzz: I want answers!

Zouric: Should I have the Kamilions begin prepara-tion for our contingency plan?

Nuzz: Yes, immediately. . . .

On the video screen Zouric squawked orders at the reptilians, who instantly filed out and marched toward the mother ship.

Klyk turned back to the kids, a look of confusion crossing over his face. "I just don't understand it."

"What don't you get?" Tara's eyebrows furrowed into a V.

"There's no way the Kamilion forces would ever work for Zouric and Nuzz. The Kamilions and the Gastropods have been fighting for two millennia," Klyk said. "Something is definitely wrong."

"What did they just tell the Kamilions to do?" TJ asked.

"I couldn't hear what he said," Klyk told them. "Something about getting the bugs ready, but I don't know what that means. . . ."

"I think it means we're in way over our heads," Tara said. "Guys, we should probably get out of here."

"Wait," Kevin said, looking at the monitor. "They're talking again."

They all listened intently as Klyk translated.

Nuzz: We need to find out what happened to Mim. One of these earthlings must know.

The alien brainiac scanned the mob of stone-still campers.

Zouric: How about that one over there? He looks like

a real know-it-all. Nuzz's mechanical legs skittered through the crowd before stopping in front of none other than Alexander Russ, Kevin's longtime science camp nemesis.

Kevin watched the screen as Zouric and Nuzz paused, looking at the nerd bully. Nuzz aimed one of its robotic limbs at Alexander and zapped him with a reverse freeze-ray.

In a flash Alexander unfroze in a state of utter panic. "Run for your lives! They're here! They're here! Run for your lives!" His voice cracked on the last word.

Nuzz's hologram face studied Alexander curiously.

Alexander caught a glimpse of the robotic brain alien standing in front of him and flinched back. He screamed like a terrified cheerleader in a horror movie.

Zouric squawked like a banshee, cutting Alexander off. The alien's mouth opened up and released a leechlike tongue that extended to about an inch from Alexander's face. The leech tongue probed the air in front of Alexander's nose. Alexander's entire body went rigid with fear, and a dark wet spot appeared around the

crotch of his pants. Kevin choked back a chuckle, realizing that his nemesis had just peed himself.

Nuzz's arm recoiled and tapped a button on its
mechanical exoskeleton. "Little tiny piece of nothing-
ness!" Nuzz shouted at Alexander in perfect English.
He must have activated some sort of neuro-lingual chip.
"Tell us everything you know, or my friend Zouric here
will turn your insides into your outsides. Am I making
myself perfectly clear? I'd be happy to go into the gory
details if you'd like. . . ."

"Uhhh, n-n-n-no." Alexander trembled. "That's
okay. I'll tell you whatever you want. Just keep the big

guy away from me."

The hologram of Nuzz's "face" faded out and a picture of Mim appeared on the glass display case protecting the brain inside. "Where is he?"

"Oh, that guy!" Alexander said, sounding a bit more like himself now. "I had nothing to do with that. I swear on my grandmother's grave, it was those other idiots."

"What other idiots?" Nuzz asked.

"Kevin Brewer, Warner Reed, TJ Boyd, and Tara Swift," Alexander named names. "I don't know that much. Everything happened real fast. He was eating up half the town like some kind of Tasmanian devil. But Kevin and the others, they're the ones you want. They zapped your friend with some kind of wormhole portal ray."

"What do these 'others' look like?" Nuzz asked.

"Here, I'll show you," Alexander said, pulling out his smartphone. "I have some pictures from when they were sneaking around at night, probably with this Mim guy. But that's all I really know, okay? So don't hurt me, all right?" He scrolled through his phone and then handed it to Nuzz.

"That little snitch!" Tara gasped, watching this all from the screen in the lab. "Why does he have pics of us on his phone?"

"Shhhh!" Warner shushed her.

"Don't shush me!" Tara said, crinkling her face up. "I'm so not the girl you want to shush. . . ."

"Both of you shush," Kevin said, focusing on the monitor. Nuzz was studying the photos and scanning them into his glass helmet's video display.

"Where are their sleeping quarters located?" Nuzz asked, and Alexander pointed to the cabin belonging to Kevin, Warner, and TJ.

"What are you doing here on Earth?" Alexander asked meekly.

Nuzz looked at Alexander coldly and said very matter-of-factly, "We're taking over your planet and enslaving every last one of you disgusting human vermin. What else would we be doing here?"

Nuzz then aimed his freeze-ray-equipped arm at Alexander and zapped him back into a human statue once again.

Suddenly, the toy car's video camera lifted off the ground, and the kids were immediately face-to-face with Zouric's ugly alien mug sneering out from the computer monitor.

It glared into the lens and its voice squawked and gabbled something incoherent. *"Grlyhfrztz harctewn prlykttnstz?"* Zouric's voice sounded like a person trying to talk while gargling mouthwash.

"What did he just say?" TJ asked.

Klyk translated for them once again. "He said that enemy spies will be fed to the reptilians when captured. . . ."

A few seconds later Nuzz's digital face appeared in the camera lens, his expression a mixture of anger and confusion.

Kevin and the gang paused in breathless silence.

"Whoever is listening," Nuzz said. "Do us a favor and tell Kevin Brewer, Warner Reed, TJ Boyd, and Tara Swift that we are coming for them."

Kevin swallowed hard, gulping down his fear.

"They can run and they can hide, but we will find

them." The camera then tilted toward the sky and crashed to the ground. The video feed cut out and the screen went fuzzy with black-and-white static.

"Aw, man," TJ said. "They just trashed our drone car!"

"Who cares about the car?" Tara said. "Those things are gonna turn us inside out!"

"I know," said TJ. "It's just a bummer the car's destroyed, that's all."

"Okay, kids," Klyk said. "Playtime's over. We have to get out of here."

"Where are we supposed to go?" Tara asked, freaking out a little. "I'm really bad at hide-and-seek,

you guys, and I'm probably gonna be even worse at hide-and-get-seeked-by-a-bunch-of-alien-lunatics!"

"Calm down, Tara," TJ said. "I'll protect you."

"No offense, Teej," Tara said, "but that doesn't exactly make me feel better."

"We're going to head back to the girls' soccer camp," Kevin said. "We'll stand a better chance over there. The freeze-ray bomb didn't reach them."

"Now you're speakin' my language," Warner said.

"Kevin, I really don't think this is the time for you guys to go gaga for some short-shorts-wearing soccer chicks," Tara said. "Even if the world is ending."

"What are you talking about?" Kevin said, looking at her funny. "We have to get away from here. And we need to warn them about what's going on! Maybe they can help."

"Yeah, you know . . . ," said Warner. "Like with our footwork and stuff."

"That's a good point," TJ said innocently. "I could use some help on my foot-eye coordination. My feet don't have any arches."

"Good story, Teej," Tara said. "Hashtag: not so much."

"Hashtag: why don't you shush up?" TJ responded.

"Hashtag: why don't you make me?" Tara said.

"Five bucks on Tara if they start fighting," Warner said. "Hashtag: sorry, TJ."

"Everybody just chill down," Kevin said. "And stop saying 'hashtag' before everything. It's super annoying."

"Are you four hashtags about ready to roll out?" Klyk asked, looking a wee bit agitated.

They hurried across the lab trailer and scurried out through the door to make a break for the woods and leave their alien-infested science camp behind.

Kevin led the pack behind the cocooned mess hall and peered around the corner, making sure to stay hidden behind the thick strands of knotted arachnopod silk. The Kamilions were gathered way on the other side of camp, near the ramp of the mother ship. Zouric and Nuzz stood before their reptilian army, barking orders at them.

Kevin noticed one of the Kamilions walking out of their bunk. The alien reptile carried some laundry baskets under his strong, scaly arm. The Kamilion minion plopped their dirty laundry down at Zouric's feet and rejoined the ranks of the reptilian army.

Nuzz plucked a T-shirt out of a basket and tossed

it into the crowd of Kamilions. "Hey, that's my favorite shirt!" Warner said as they all watched the reptilian aliens sniff their unwashed clothes.

"Ick!" Tara clamped her hand over her mouth to stifle a squeal as Nuzz pulled out a pair of Kevin's boxer shorts. "They're smelling you guys' underwear! What a bunch of sickos!"

"They're giving them your scent so they can better hunt you down," Klyk said.

Kevin didn't like the sound of a bunch of Kamilions knowing his scent.

A small lens on the waist of Nuzz's robotic body flickered and flashed. The air in front of him lit up with a hologram. Perfect three-dimensional images of the four of them floated in the air. The reptilians studied the holograms of the kids closely, memorizing their faces before breaking off in search parties.

Kevin, Warner, Tara, and TJ were officially the most wanted humans in the galaxy.

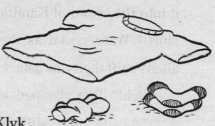

"Quick, get down!" Klyk ordered them back behind the corner of the mess hall and out of sight. Their mini alien friend pointed to a crawl space between the outer wall of the mess hall and the web of arachnopod silk. The four of them dropped down and huddled together under the cover of the arachnopod's webbing.

"What are you freaking out about?" Warner asked as he stooped down last to hide from view. "They can't see us from here."

"Hurry, get in!" Klyk shouted at them. "They're coming!"

"Klyk, I don't see anyone coming," Tara said, looking out through the space between the strands of the arachnopod's cocoon.

Kevin peered through the alien web, too, and suddenly saw what Klyk was talking about.

Two reptilian figures were indeed moving toward them. Only they didn't look quite like themselves. It was as if the Kamilions walking toward them were made up of light particles that camouflaged their reptilian skin against whatever environment surrounded them.

"That's their natural camouflage," Klyk whispered to them.

The reptilian duo blended into the blue-green tint of the freeze-rayed forest.

Kevin looked across the terrain. The pine forest was only a short distance away. They had to make a run for it right now.

"Everybody, go-go-go!" Klyk shouted, and they all scurried out from under the fort of arachnopod silk. Running as fast as they could, the five of them disappeared into the forest, zigzagging through the pine trees.

On the other side of the woods, they all dashed out again onto the soccer fields, unseen by the prowling reptilian guard. They slowed to a halt in front of the all-girls sports camp's large field house. The sports facility seemed out of place in the middle of the wilderness, more like a building on a high school campus. The double doors had been propped open, and Kevin poked his head into the gym.

"Hey, Warner," Tara said. "What happened to your backpack?"

Warner groaned as he realized he'd left it back in the robotics lab trailer. He slapped his forehead with the palm of his hand. "Ugh! I always do that!"

"We had, like, almost our entire arsenal of weapons in that bag!" TJ groaned.

"Whatever," Warner said defensively. "All that stuff was out of power anyway."

"Except for the de-atomizer ray," Tara sniped.

"Come on, we'll figure it out later," Kevin said. "Let's go."

Kevin stepped through the doors after Warner. Once inside, a wave of sweltering heat struck the four of them. Kevin glanced around the field house. Roving clusters of teenage girls gathered in one great hectic, chaotic, sweaty mass that filled up the entire gym.

Even with the daylight coming through the skylights, the gym was dim from the blackout that Mim had caused a few hours earlier when he ate all the telephone and power lines and devoured the nearby cell phone towers. Kevin recalled the sick feeling he got when he realized they were disconnected from the outside world.

Inside the gymnasium, a big industrial-sized electric fan sat idle by the doorway, powerless to stir the muggy air.

At least two hundred girls milled around chitchatting, fanning each other with magazines, and juggling soccer balls on their knees.

They all wore cleats with knee-high socks over shin guards, mesh shorts, and T-shirts with the sleeves rolled up. Some of the girls sat on the floor braiding each other's hair. A few others lay on their backs, sprawled out, barely able to take the heat.

Walking through the groups of campers, a trio of junior counselors, maybe eighteen years old, tried to settle everyone down.

"Okay, everybody chill!" a tall blond girl wearing a pair of Umbros and Adidas cleats yelled to the rest of the camp through a megaphone. Her voice echoed off the walls of the indoor athletic complex.

A voice called out from the throng of tweenaged soccer campers: "How are we supposed to chill when it's, like, a hundred degrees in here?"

"A little heat never killed anyone," yelled the girl with the megaphone.

Not true, Kevin thought, a bit shocked at the level of misinformation being dispensed here. People died from heatstroke all the time because they weren't careful.

"Everybody pipe down and listen up!" the megaphone girl blurted through the speaker. The soccer campers stopped what they were doing and took seats on the hardwood floor. The chatter quieted down to a dull mumble.

The blond girl with the megaphone waited for complete silence before she started to talk. "Coach Jones and some of the other counselors went over to the science camp across the lake to see if the geek squad knows anything about what happened to the electricity and the wireless internet connection."

"Ahem." Kevin cleared his throat nervously. "Excuse me. . . ." He could feel his blood throbbing to the beat of his pulse. His face flushed a bright beet-red color that most likely clashed with his orange hair. Megaphone Girl swiveled her head toward Kevin, Warner, Tara, and TJ, who were now the only ones still standing.

"Can we help you?" she asked.

Kevin and the gang stood awkwardly amid the sea of soccer camp girls.

"My name's K-Kevin," he stuttered. "And we're from Northwest Horizons."

"Is that supposed to mean something to me?"

"It's the science camp across the lake, sweetie," Tara said sassily, cocking her head to one side with a little bit of an attitude. "You know, the one with all the smart people who are going to run the world one day?"

"Oh, you guys are nerdcampers?" said the girl

with the megaphone. "Why didn't you say so in the first place?" She then turned to Tara. "And don't call me sweetie, *sweetie*. . . ."

Tara crossed her arms defiantly and twisted her face into a scrunched-up stink-eye.

"Okay, so are you guys going to fix the internet or what?" One of Megaphone Girl's sidekicks shot them an impatient look and held up her smartphone. "My boyfriend is probably trying to text me right now."

"You guys have to listen up," Kevin said. "The internet is the least of our worries right now!"

"Yeah," TJ said. "A bunch of really bad aliens who want to take over the world just landed in our backyard."

The all-girls camp was quiet for a moment, then everyone burst out with a rip-roar of laughter.

"Seriously, you guys need to listen to us," Warner said. "It's not safe here!"

"Do you really expect us to believe that there are aliens out there right now?" the megaphone blared at them.

"Fine, you want us to prove it?" Kevin said, reaching

into his bag. He held Klyk up for everyone to see. "I give you Klyk!"

But their little alien pal was stiff as a board, not moving a muscle.

The gaggle of soccer girls started to giggle.

"Aw, that's so adorable," one of the girls said. "He thinks the toy's real!"

"Klyk, what are you doing?" Kevin said out of the corner of his mouth. "Say something."

Staying as still as could be, Klyk flicked his eyes and gazed at Kevin, then whispered, "What do you suspect would happen if these girls actually thought the world was being taken over by aliens?"

"I don't know," Kevin said. "Help us kick alien butt?"

"That's kind of what they're good at," TJ said. "I'm sure butts are just as easy to kick as soccer balls . . . maybe even easier."

"Wrong," Klyk said. "They're going to flip out and cause a rumpus of unwanted attention. . . ."

"Did you just use the word 'rumpus'?" Warner looked puzzled.

"He's right, Kev," said Tara. "I'm not so sure this group is mentally prepared for the fact that life exists on other planets. We're wasting our time here."

A little bit agitated, Kevin tossed Klyk in the backpack.

"Hey! What are you—" Klyk shouted as Kevin zipped up the pocket, muffling his miniature alien friend's protest.

"You're just a toy, remember?" he said. "You're not supposed to talk."

Kevin watched as Megaphone Girl turned back to the rest of the camp, forgetting about them completely and moving along with their daily soccer routine. "Come on, ladies! Everybody line up in your assigned groups. We're not going to let a little blackout stop us from doing our stations, are we? On the double, ladies, let's go!"

As the soccer campers rose from the floor and

exited the field house, Kevin, Warner, TJ, and Tara were left in the middle of the gym.

Kevin hung his head, crestfallen, as they all walked out of the gym. What were they supposed to do now? They couldn't just waltz back to camp and fight off all those Kamilions. That wasn't going to work. No, Kevin was quite sure they had to be much sneakier about it than that. They didn't have enough information to solve the problem. It was like one of those multiple-choice questions you couldn't know the answer to.

The lone clippity-clop of someone's soccer cleats echoed down the hall behind them. They all spun around as one of the soccer campers caught up to them and stopped.

Her hair was bright red and curly. She had sparkly green eyes and a face full of freckles. A multicolored goalie jersey clung to her torso, and a pair of black mesh shorts hung down past her kneecaps. Kevin guessed she could probably do at least forty push-ups without breaking a sweat.

Kevin found himself a little jittery. He got nervous

talking to almost any girl—aside from Tara, of course, but she was cool—and this particular one looked like she could manhandle the four of them with no problem whatsoever.

Kevin stepped forward and stuck out his hand, and she clasped it with a firm grip. "I'm Kevin Brewer," he said to her, and gestured to his friends. "And this is Warner. That's Tara. And that's TJ."

"Sup." She nodded at the gang. "I'm Marcy."

"Hey, Marcy," Warner, Tara, and TJ all said in unison.

"Okay," said Marcy. She seemed a little frazzled, out of sorts, like something was weighing on her mind. "Will one of you please tell me I'm not completely crazy?"

"I mean, we just met," TJ said. "For all we know, you might be totally bonkers."

"I've seen some weird stuff going on the past few days," she said. "I tried to report it to the head counselors, but they told me I was probably just suffering from heatstroke." Marcy paused for a beat. "But it wasn't heatstroke."

"What kind of stuff have you seen?" Warner asked.

"Down by the lake the other night I saw some nasty-looking octo-spiderpus thing. I thought my mind was playing tricks on me. But then the next day I saw some little purple fuzzy guy when I was on a nature hike between scrimmages, and I knew it had to be aliens. They look exactly like the characters in this Max Greyson comic book I have."

Just then, Klyk unzipped Kevin's bag, climbed out, and perched on his shoulder. "You're not imagining things, Marcy. Everything you've seen is real."

Marcy pointed at Klyk with an awestruck look on her face. "That thing's talking! What is that thing?"

"It's not a thing," TJ explained. "It's a him. He's an alien space cop and his name is Klyk."

"It's so cool!" Marcy said. "He's so little."

"Wait a second." Warner stopped Marcy. "What did you just say about Max Greyson?"

"I'm only, like, his number one fan," she said.

"But what comic did you see Mim and the arachnopod in?" said Warner. "They haven't been part of the series."

Her eyes narrowed and she gave the group a once-over. "I have something to show you guys. Come with me."

Kevin and his friends hustled after Marcy across
the practice field. She led them to the main housing cabin, a longhouse-style building. The four of them
filed inside and followed Marcy down the alley between
two rows of bunk beds. The interior of the cabin was set
up like a military barracks. The beds were all perfectly
made and everything was exceedingly tidy. Someone
was running a tight ship.

"The girl back there said your coaches were heading toward our camp—do you remember how long ago
they left?" Kevin glanced out the window to scope the
campgrounds for any alien threats.

"Not that long," she said, checking the clock on the

wall. "Maybe, like, half an hour ago?"

"Maybe they got hit by the freeze-ray bomb," TJ offered up a hypothesis.

"Maybe . . . ," Kevin said, biting his bottom lip in thought.

"What do you mean, freeze-ray bomb?" Marcy said, stopping in front of one of the bunk beds. "Are they okay?"

"We don't know yet," Warner said. "They could be absolutely fine, they could be freeze-rayed, or they could be having their insides turned into their outsides."

"Is that supposed to make me feel better?" Marcy scowled at Warner.

"Marcy, don't listen to him. He doesn't know what he's talking about," Kevin said. "They're fine, I'm sure. Now, what were you going to show us?"

"Oh, that's right!" Marcy said. "I almost forgot."

Kevin, Warner, Tara, and TJ stood in a semicircle around Marcy as she knelt down and slid out a cardboard box from beneath the bed frame. "Here we go," Marcy said, and opened the file box to reveal a twin stack of sci-fi and fantasy books.

"Whoa, you got a *Brainstorm #1*?" Warner said, picking up a comic book out of the box. "Mine's all beat-up, but this one is mint condition!"

"I know, and I intend to keep it that way," said Marcy nervously. "So please be careful."

"What did you say you wanted to show us, Marcy?" Tara said.

"This," she said, sifting through the box and producing a comic titled *The Wrath of Mim*. "It's where I recognized Mim and the arachnopod from."

"Huh?" Warner's eyes lit up. "Let me see that!" He nearly ripped it out of Marcy's hand he was so excited. "How do I not know about this?"

"It's a special-edition, limited-release issue I got through the *Brainstorm* fan club."

"I didn't even know there was a fan club!" Warner said. His jaw

dropped at this never-before-seen issue.

"Oh, you should totally join," said Marcy. "It's awesome! You get all kinds of stuff for free: T-shirts, trading cards, action figures, and of course special editions."

Kevin, Tara, and TJ leaned over Warner's shoulder as he flipped to page one of *The Wrath of Mim*. The comic began with a picture of a futuristic city on a distant planet. The next panel showed Mim on the outskirts of the alien metropolis during one of his crazed states of mass consumption. The third panel illustrated the city, reduced to rubble, after being decimated by their former "friend," the purple planet-eater.

On the next page the comic revealed Mim licking his chops on the now-barren planet. The only thing left was an arachnopod. Kevin recognized the creature as Mim's pet,

Poobah, who they had taken down earlier that day. The illustration showed Mim trying to eat the alien, but as soon as he got close, Poobah sprayed him with a dark, inky spittle that made Mim gag. "YUCK!" A little thought bubble appeared over Mim's cartoon head on the next panel. "I don't feel good. This creature is poison. . . . I will make him my guard pet instead." The following page showed Mim taking the arachnopod in as his pet.

Kevin looked up at Marcy. "No wonder the galactascope worked!" he said. "Everything in the comic book is turning out to be real!"

"You know how crazy that sounds, don't you?" Marcy said, raising an eyebrow.

"You'd be surprised what our last few days have been like," Tara said.

"We need more information than this," Klyk said from his perch on Kevin's shoulder. "Mim and Poobah are old news."

"Have you ever read anything about a couple of aliens named Zouric and Nuzz?" TJ asked Marcy.

The soccer goalie looked at the ceiling and scratched her temple, thinking for a moment. "Nope, not ringing any bells."

"We have to find out what's really going on," Kevin said.

"If only we could talk to Max Greyson in person . . . ," Tara said. "I mean, if he knew all about Mim, maybe he would know about Zouric and Nuzz, too."

"That would be awesome," Warner said. "But fair warning, guys—don't be offended when Max and I become best friends, okay?"

"Well, then, why don't you just go to his house?" Marcy said.

"Nobody even knows where he lives," Warner said. "He's very secretive about his private life."

"Not that secretive." Marcy pulled out an envelope stuck between the pages of one of the comic books. "Max Greyson lives in Colorado. I have his address. I wrote him a fan letter once a couple of years ago and he wrote me back. See?"

She handed Kevin the envelope with the address written on it.

"How are we supposed to get to Colorado?" TJ asked.

"We still have my space cruiser," Klyk said. "It has the invisibility shield on. They probably don't even know it's there. . . . If we can get to the ship, it can take us anywhere on Earth pretty quickly."

"How fast does your spaceship travel?" Kevin asked.

"About a mile per second," Klyk told them.

"Okay, we're about a thousand miles away from Denver." Kevin did some quick math in his head. "That means we can make it there in 16.6667 minutes."

"And we can use my ship's communication system to request backup," Klyk added. "Call in the cavalry and wait for reinforcements."

"How are we going to find your ship?" Kevin asked the mini-alien.

Klyk tapped the side of his head where the robotic eyepiece was embedded into his skull. "I can see the ship with my biotech. I can lead the way. . . ."

"Then that's that," Warner said. "We have to get to Klyk's ship if we're going to have any chance at beating Zouric and Nuzz."

"You mean we have to go back into the alien freak zone?" Tara asked.

"I don't think we have a choice," TJ said. "Do you?"

"There's just one other thing," said Klyk. "One of you is going to have to fly the ship. I'm a little too little right now, but I can guide you through it."

"I call driver's seat," Warner said quickly, jumping at the thought of getting behind the controls of a real alien spaceship.

"Then let's get out of here," Kevin said. "If we're going to throw a kink in Zouric and Nuzz's plans, then every second's going to count."

"I don't know what you guys are talking about, but do you mind if I come along?" Marcy asked. "This all sounds really awesome."

"Of course," Kevin said. "We need all the help we can get!"

As they were getting ready to leave, a pair of foot-steps clomped outside the cabin and someone knocked on the door with a rap-a-tap-tap.

"Who is it?" Marcy asked, creeping across the

cabin. She peered through a crack in the wooden door, then turned around and whispered to Kevin and the gang, "It's my counselor. . . ."

The counselor's voice resounded behind the door. "Kevin Brewer, Warner Reed, Tara Swift, and TJ Boyd must be located."

"Hold on one sec," Marcy said, and gave Kevin a strange look. "That's weird. She's asking for you guys."

"Why would she know who we are?" TJ asked.

"She wouldn't," said Tara.

The counselor banged on the door again, only this time much, much harder.

"Just a minute," Marcy said, trying to stall.

"Unsatisfactory," the counselor said in a robotic voice. "All campers must report for processing immediately."

"That's weird," said Marcy. "She doesn't sound like herself. . . ."

"What was she saying about processing?" TJ asked.

"Maybe that's what Zouric and Nuzz were talking about," Tara said. "What if they're using some kind of mind control or something. . . ."

"Why would they want to do that?" Kevin asked.

"Because it'll be that much easier to take over the planet," Klyk said, "if you guys are a bunch of mindless automatons."

"All campers must report for processing immediately," the dull monotone voice repeated.

Alien brain processing? Kevin thought. *Thanks, but no thanks.*

Bam-bam-bam! Three loud knocks rapped on the door followed by three more. *Bam-bam-bam!* The hinges shook, and the wood around the door frame started to splinter as the robo-counselor began to kick the door down.

Wham-crack! The brainwashed counselor's arm exploded through the center panel of the door like a karate master punching through a block of wood. She reached her arm through the jagged opening and twisted the doorknob with a click. The door creaked open, and Marcy's soccer counselor stood in the doorway, her chest heaving, breathing heavily through her nostrils like a raging bull. Bright red lines of fresh blood trickled down the knuckles on her hand, a fact she seemed to care nothing about. The counselor's ink-black eyes seemed to scan all their faces.

"Whereabouts located," her robotic voice intoned. "All earthlings must report for processing."

"Fat chance, lady!" TJ said, grabbing a pillow off one of the bunk beds. He cranked it back, holding the

pillowcase tightly, and drilled the brainwashed soccer counselor in the side of her head.

POW!

Her head snapped to one side but she didn't budge an inch. Kevin squinted through his glasses and stared at the counselor's neck. He could see a swollen puncture wound at the nape that resembled a giant spider bite.

The soccer coach glared down at TJ. Her blank, glossed-over eyes shuttered down to black alien irises. TJ dropped the pillow on the cabin floor and squealed, jumping back to hide behind Marcy.

"You wanna play rough?" Tara said, and pulled out the telepathy helmet from Kevin's backpack. She placed it on her head and hit the power switch, training her gaze on the soccer camp counselor. The alien psychic technology flashed with brainwave energy and pulsed with a mechanical hum.

The brainwashed counselor froze in the doorway, unable to move, caught between two conflicting neural impulses. Tara focused all her mental strength on the soccer coach.

Kevin, Warner, TJ, and Marcy scurried past the counselor. They all jumped down off the steps of the cabin and hit the ground running, making a beeline for the border of the forest across the way.

"Tara, come on!" Kevin shouted, doubling back to wait for his teammate lagging behind. "Let's go!" But Tara was still standing locked in a psychic trance with the brainwashed soccer counselor. "Tara!" Kevin shouted again, and watched as the telepathy helmet started to go haywire on top of Tara's head.

The lights on the alien headpiece spewed sparks and the motor emitted an awful sound like silverware in a garbage disposal.

Tara's eyes rolled to the back of her skull, and Kevin raced to her aid. Taking hold of the helmet, he tugged at it hard with both hands. The mind-reading device came loose and shocked Kevin with such force that the volt of electricity surged up his arms and sent him back reeling against the wall.

Tara and the soccer counselor collapsed together in the aftermath of their mental standoff. Kevin popped back up and shook the shock from his arms. It stung pretty badly, but he was okay. He rushed over to Tara's side and helped her to her feet as she came out of the trance.

"Tara?" Kevin asked her. "You all right?"

"I could see it!" she cried. "I could see what they're going to do!"

Kevin looked up as the soccer counselor rose from a slumped heap on the floor and blocked the doorway. Tara snapped to attention and bolted forward, diving between the counselor's legs and scampering out the door.

"Kevin Brewer must be captured," the counselor said in a monotone. "Kevin Brewer must be captured." She lifted her arms and grabbed him.

"Not today," Kevin said, and picked up the pillow TJ had dropped and slugged the counselor in the back of her knees. The brainwashed soccer coach fell down and lost her grip on Kevin, who took off after Tara, slamming the door shut behind him.

The two of them sprinted toward the edge of the woods and caught up with Warner, TJ, and Marcy. Together, the five of them along with Klyk tiptoed slyly through the woods back toward Northwest Horizons, on the lookout for the Kamilion guard. Dirt and twigs crunched beneath their feet. Their footsteps grew silent as they entered the outer circumference of the freeze-ray bomb's blast area.

"What happened back there?" Warner asked.

"It was awful," Tara said, pinching the skin between her eyebrows. "Zouric and Nuzz are going to brainwash everyone."

"How are they going to do it?" TJ asked. "Could you see it?"

"I'm not sure," she said, wincing as she tried to picture what she had seen while strapped into the telepathy helmet. "It was something to do with—"

"Ouch!" Marcy cried out suddenly, and grabbed the back of her neck.

"What is it, Marcy?" Kevin asked.

"Something bit me!" She breathed in and out quickly, starting to hyperventilate.

An electronic buzz droned in the air. Something about the size of a hummingbird fluttered in the corner of Kevin's eye. Its face had a long metallic needle protruding like the snout of a large mosquito.

The alien robot bug levitated to and fro overhead, ready to strike.

Marcy stood stock-still, clasping the nape of her neck where the robotic bug had stung her. Her hand

then flopped
down to the side,
and her neck hung
with her chin touching her
chest. A few seconds later,
her head lifted up, and her eyes were
glassy, blank, and evil.

"Kevin Brewer must be captured," droned Marcy.

"She's one of them now!" TJ shouted.

"Duck!" Tara cried. "That alien bug is coming right at us!"

The nanobug dive-bombed the group, and they all flinched away, batting at the air as it buzzed around their heads. It landed on the back of Kevin's neck, and he felt its legs pricking his skin. He swatted the extraterrestrial pest to the ground before it could puncture the skin.

The mechanical insect floundered in the dirt with a broken wing, unable to resume its aerial attack. The insecto-bot leaked out a batch of bluish goo from a synthetic pouch located on its underbelly. Kevin bent over and studied the blue alien fluid. The liquid churned in the dirt, wriggling around as if it had somewhere better, more productive to be.

"It's like this stuff has a mind of its own," Kevin observed. "It must be some kind of super-sophisticated nanotechnology. You know, like microscopic robots that can be introduced into a person's bloodstream."

"Thanks, Kev," said Tara. "I think we all know

what nanotechnology is. . . ."

"That's what Zouric and Nuzz must be using on the Kamilions," said Warner. "Probably some sort of mind-control nanoserum."

"Their nanoscience must be really advanced," Kevin said, turning to Klyk. "Do you know anything about it?"

"I'm no scientist," said Klyk. "But Zouric and Nuzz are wanted for stealing top secret military technology from the interplanetary alliance."

"Hmm." TJ thought about that for a moment, examining the fallen nanobug. "It must inject into the spinal cord, which allows them to take over the host's brain function. . . ."

"That makes sense," said Klyk. "It's the only reason why the Kamilions would be taking orders from those two scuzzbuckets."

"This is bad, you guys," Warner said. "We have to get to Max Greyson's house as soon as possible."

"Hey," Tara said. "Where did Marcy go?"

Kevin looked around for their new friend, but she

was nowhere in sight. In the distance, a high-pitched whistle screeched through the thick, hot summer air. The four of them whipped their heads around.

Kevin spotted Marcy between two pine trees near the edge of the forest, calling her fellow soccer campers

over to follow her. The entire all-girls soccer camp was jogging across the fields toward the woods, their eyes as black as Marcy's.

They were coming right for them.

Kevin bolted away from the herd of brainwashed soccer campers. He darted through the trees, which were still frozen stiff from the freeze-ray bomb detonation. A light wind whistled through the forest, but the foliage and treetops stayed motionless in the slight breeze. Their footsteps were silent, too, as they sprinted over the solid terrain.

Kevin stopped at the edge of the clearing, panting heavily, out of breath. The fire pit was still warm from their Invention Convention celebration. The graham cracker box lay on its side, spilling crumbs onto the ground beside an open bag of marshmallows now covered in a colony of tiny red ants. Next to the s'mores ingredients, three of their former counselors—Nick, Cody, and Bailey—were still prisoners in the blocks of plasma Klyk and his bounty hunter friends had mistakenly shot them with the night before.

Warner, Tara, and TJ jogged over next to their team leader, huffing and puffing as well. They had to move fast. The brainwashed camp of soccer girls would be there in less than a minute.

"My spaceship's right there." Klyk perched on Kevin's shoulder and pointed to an empty space straight over their heads.

Kevin tilted his head back. The treetop peaked no less than thirty feet off the ground.

"How are we supposed to get up there?" Tara asked.

"Anybody got a jet pack?" Warner asked sarcastically.

"Looks like we're going to have to climb," Kevin said.

TJ looked nervous. "I've never climbed a tree before."

"Me neither," Warner said. "Not a huge fan of this outdoorsy stuff."

"Ditto . . . ," said Tara.

"Come on," Kevin said incredulously. "You guys never climbed a tree?"

His three friends shook their heads no.

Suddenly, out of the trees shot a soccer ball. It sailed through the air and drilled TJ in the side of the head. The kids whirled around and squinted into the forest thicket. More than a hundred brainwashed girl soccer campers charged toward the clearing, ready to capture them and bring them to Zouric and Nuzz.

"Well"—Kevin shrugged—"there's a first time for everything."

Warner cracked his neck to one side and jogged in place, limbering up for the climb. Tara took two awkward steps and jumped, grabbing onto the lowest tree branch. She did a chin-up, swung her leg over, and then stood up. Warner hopped up next, and then Kevin gave TJ a boost onto the first branch of the pine tree. With Klyk on his shoulder, Kevin clambered up last

and they started
their climb,
one branch at
a time.

"See that
big branch
way up
there?" Klyk
pointed up
the trunk. "We
need to get up
there. That's
where the
ladder is!"

Midway up
the tree, Kevin
looked down
from the bird's-
eye view. Big
mistake. The brain-
washed soccer

campers and their counselors emerged from the tree line and filled up the clearing.

Marcy stood at the front of the pack, staring up at Kevin.

Kevin locked eyes with their new friend turned alien brainwashee.

"Over here! Target located and locked," droned Marcy.

Kevin swiveled his head in the direction of the science camp. On the other side of the clearing, two duos of reptilian guardsmen prowled toward him. They stepped out of the woods, gazing up at Kevin and his pals.

The brainwashed soccer girls surrounded the base of the tree trunk. The Kamilions pushed through the crowd of soccer campers and positioned themselves beneath the tree, aiming their photon blasters straight up the trunk.

PYOO! PYOO! The laser beams streaked upward through the tree branches. The first blast whizzed by them and grazed Kevin's shorts, singeing the fabric. The second shot missed them completely and nailed a hefty branch in an explosion of freeze-rayed tree bark.

"Don't look down!" Klyk yelled. "Keep going!"

Careful to lift their chins up, Kevin, Warner, TJ, and Tara started to step out onto a limb of the pine.

"Out there," Klyk said, gesturing toward the end of the tree's limb. He activated the computer connected to his eye to detect the invisibility shield concealing the spacecraft. "You can grab the ladder from there."

"What ladder?" Kevin asked, looking out toward the end of the branch.

"You'll come to it. Trust me," Klyk said, straining to be heard over the girls and photon blasts below.

Kevin shim mied out cautiously to the end of the branch, maintain- ing his balance like a tightrope walker.

His foot hit a knot in the tree bark and he wobbled to the side, leaning to catch himself. He righted his posture and regained his balance. "Phew!" Kevin gasped and wiped the sweat from his brow with the back of his hand.

"Okay, now," the little alien said into Kevin's ear. "The drop ladder should be hanging right in front of you."

"Should be?" Kevin asked.

"You just want us to drop off this branch and grab onto an invisible ladder with nothing to break our fall?" Warner asked. "Are you nuts?"

"You must trust me," Klyk begged them. "There are people on your planet who don't believe in aliens because they haven't ever seen one. But that does not mean they do not exist."

Kevin peered down at the brainwashed mob crowding beneath them.

Two of the soccer camp girls had started to climb the tree, moving steadily from one branch to the next.

PYOO! PYOO! PYOO! Three more shots zipped

right past Kevin's head. "Whoa!" Kevin ducked and crouched on the branch, almost knocking into Tara, who stood behind him.

"Hey, watch it." Tara reached out and steadied herself, clutching Kevin's backpack. "Wait a minute. Hold still," she said, unzipping the bag and rummaging around. She then pulled out a can of black spray paint from when she designed the logo for the galactascope. "It's okay. You can say it."

Warner looked at her funny. "Say what?"

"How smart I am." She smirked.

Tara took the can and aimed the nozzle where Klyk had just told them the ladder was hanging. Black mist dusted the invisible ladder and a few seconds later they could make out the rungs dangling in front of them.

"That was pretty smart, Tara." TJ gave her a fist bump.

"It's a tough job." She smiled. "But someone's got to do it."

"I didn't know bragging was considered a job," Warner joked.

"Guys, come on, let's get out of here!" Kevin reached from the branch and grabbed the now visible rungs. He scaled the ladder first, with Klyk clinging to his pack, followed by Tara, then Warner, and finally TJ.

It looked like they were levitating in thin air, climbing up toward the sky. All Kevin could see were the tops of the trees and the Oregon wilderness splayed out for miles. It would have been beautiful had he not glanced over his right shoulder and seen Zouric and Nuzz's alien mother ship hovering ominously over their science camp. Kevin reached the top rung and, following Klyk's directions, pulled himself into the unseen hatch of the invisible spaceship.

A few steps later, Kevin was inside a super-high-tech space shuttle. Tara, Warner, and TJ crawled in next and they all stood up inside the spaceship.

The interior gleamed with panels of polished silver. The driver's seat sat front and center before a large rect-angular windshield with a panoramic view close to 180 degrees. A transparent touch screen hung down in front of the seat from the vaulted dome ceiling. To the rear of the saucer-shaped craft, three large, fancy computer screens were situated in front of three copilot seats, one facing due south and the other two facing east and west.

"Whoa! This thing is sweet!" Warner jumped into the pilot seat at the front of the space cruiser. "What do I do?"

"Hit that metal switch and push up that lever," Klyk said. Warner did as he was told, and the spacecraft rumbled to life.

Klyk showed Warner the control panel. There was a shiny silver joystick next to the armrest. "That controls the thrust of the engine. Forward is go. If you pull back you'll stop.

"Now, by your left hand, that sphere is for your palm to control steering and maneuvering," Klyk told him. "That button on your right is for the invisibility shield. The one next to it will activate the force field. Both of them can't be on at the same time."

ZVRF! ZVRF! ZVRF! Three ray gun blasts pelted the side of the spacecraft. The alien machinery to the left of the steering column flashed with bright orange sparks and started to smoke.

"The communication system!" Klyk shouted in anguish. "Activate the force field!"

Warner tapped the button, and the force field activated.

Kevin could feel the technological pulse enveloping

the entire ship.

Marcy and three other soc- cer camp girls now climbed the pine tree, only one branch away from the spray-painted ladder. Kevin bent

down and pulled the ladder up out of reach as three more reptilian laser blasts whizzed past his arm.

ZVRF! ZVRF! ZVRF!

Kevin looked down and squinted through his glasses. On the ground below them, two figures appeared at the fringe of the forest thicket: Zouric and Nuzz. Kevin gasped as Zouric sprang into action. The long, Gumby-like alien slug-man strode through the horde of his brainwashed subjects and bounded off his thin, lean, gelatinous legs with an impressive eight-foot vertical leap.

"Get us out of here, Warner!" Kevin shouted over the zip-zap sounds zinging through the air. "This guy's got some serious hops!"

Zouric cat-leaped past the soccer girls halfway up the trunk and swung on a large pinewood branch, flipping around completely as if he were a gymnast on a set of uneven bars. He then flung himself airborne and reached for the spacecraft. His alien fingers stretched, ready to latch onto the metal edge along the alien ship's exterior. Kevin heard a clunk as the gigantic Gastropod grabbed onto the force field surrounding their spacecraft instead.

"Warner, do something!" Tara shouted, watching Zouric pulling himself up onto their spaceship. "Get rid of him!"

"No problem," Warner said, flipping the steering controls. "He doesn't know who he's messing with."

Warner shifted the lever and angled the spacecraft, twisting his palm slightly on the steering sphere. The spaceship jerked side to side, one wing dipping back and forth and then the other. Zouric lost his grip, barely holding on with one hand while trying to sling his other arm back up.

Warner then flipped the steering controls and the spaceship spun 360 degrees before coming to a dead stop above the treetops. Zouric yowled and went flying into the trees.

"Way to go, Warner!" Kevin cheered.

"Go, Warner, it's your birthday," TJ said, and did a little celebration dance.

"It's not my birthday," Warner said, shifting gears.

The spacecraft rose swiftly above the treetops and then jolted to a stop high above Zouric and Nuzz's brain-washed army of reptilians and soccer campers.

"I know it's not your birthday," TJ said. "It's just an expression."

Warner chuckled and hit the throttle on the steering column. "Whatever's clever, my man."

The spaceship shot forward and they were off full throttle for Colorado, soaring far away from their alien-infested science camp.

Klyk's spaceship pierced the overcast sky and shot out of the clouds as it cruised into the stratosphere.

"Yee haw!" Warner hollered as he accelerated into hyperdrive. They flew through the clear blue sky as if they were the wind itself. The craft didn't really seem to be moving, Kevin thought. It felt more like they were stationary and the Earth was rotating faster and faster beneath them.

Klyk scaled the wall up to the interstellar communication device that had short-circuited during the firefight.

"It's dead," Klyk said, punching the power button in frustration.

"Can you fix it?" Tara asked.

"I can try," Klyk said, turning back to the alien communication device. "But it's not looking good."

Kevin stood in front of the navigation system next to Warner. "Hey, Klyk, how do I input the address we got from Marcy?"

Klyk jumped up on the armrest on Warner's seat at the main controls. "Push the button on the left and then you can access the local network and google whatever info you need."

"You know what Google is?" Tara asked, futzing around with one of the three firing stations located around the rear of the craft.

"You don't seriously think humans invented Google, do you?" Klyk said.

Kevin looked up the precise latitude and longitude for Max Greyson's house and punched the coordinates into the spaceship's guidance system.

Warner put the spaceship on autopilot and kicked his feet up on the control board. As they flew toward the Rocky Mountains, Klyk grunted and grumbled to himself, trying to fix their communications.

"How does it look, Klyk? Any chance we're going to be able to call for backup?" Kevin asked him.

"The whole system's shot," Klyk said. "There's no way to fix it. Looks like we're on our own."

Kevin felt a knot in his stomach tighten. He knew it had sounded too good to be true that they could get out of this mess by calling for reinforcements. Zouric and Nuzz were their problem and their problem alone. Nobody could stop these alien creeps now except for Kevin and his friends.

"Klyk, get over here quick!" Warner said, sitting back up in the pilot seat abruptly. "Check this out. I think we've got some company."

The little cyborg hopped across the control board and looked at the radar screen. Two red flashing triangles were homing in on their ship.

"Enemy space cruisers," Klyk said.

"Are you sure?" TJ asked. "Maybe it's the air force or something. I bet we could fly circles around them!"

"Those aren't fighter jets," Klyk said. "They're moving too fast."

"Zouric and Nuzz?" Tara asked.

"Probably just a couple of Kamilions."

"Just?" Kevin said, but Klyk ignored him.

"Warner, are you ready for this?" Klyk asked his pilot. "You're going to have to do some fancy flying to lose these guys."

"Are you kidding me?" Warner said, glancing at the reptilian cruisers. "I was born for this."

"What do we do?" Kevin asked.

"Kevin, Tara, TJ." Klyk ordered them to the co-pilot seats. "Man the photon blasters while I activate the viewports."

Kevin, Tara, and TJ hustled over and each sat before one of the three firing stations facing the rear of the ship. The stations looked like arcade games with screens showing a live video feed from the exterior of the cruising ship.

They waited until Klyk flicked on the viewports and the screens flashed to life. Kevin could see the clouds whipping by and a Kamilion cruiser drifting into the frame. The reptilian spacecraft looked mean, like the jaw and pincers of a desert beetle.

"Fire at will!" Klyk shouted.

Kevin grabbed the control stick and lined up the enemy spacecraft in the digital crosshairs on the video monitor.

Kevin pulled the trigger, and two photon blasts streaked past the target and disappeared against the bright blue sky.

The pair of Kamilion cruisers flew in tandem behind them, trailing from a slightly higher angle than Klyk's spaceship.

Warner twisted the steering sphere with a flick of his wrist, and they dipped down beneath the cruisers. Warner then switched directions suddenly in the air,

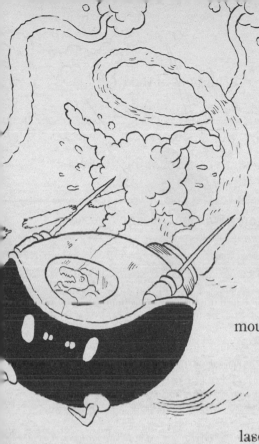

and the alien cruisers flew past. The Kamilions made a sharp U-turn to keep up with Klyk's ship.

"Yeah, yeah," Warner shouted. "Gotcha!" He swerved around a snowcapped mountain peak as the alien cruisers adjusted their course.

ZAP! ZAP! Two laser blasts struck the force field as the cruisers kept pace with Klyk's spaceship.

"Lower us down into the mountain range," Klyk instructed him. "We have more agility than these guys. We might be able to lose them in the valleys."

Warner steered them lower, and they sailed through a narrow gorge in the valley flanked by two mountainsides. He weaved in and out of the laser blasts as they cruised ten feet above the valley floor.

"The gameplay on this thing is incredible!" Warner said, flipping the steering sphere and pushing the hyperdrive to its limits.

"It's not a video game, Warner," Kevin reminded him.

"I don't know, Kev," he said. "It sure feels like one."

"Slow down," Klyk commanded Warner. "You won't be able to bank at that speed." Warner eased up and the spacecraft steadied.

Swoomp! Swoomp! The reptilian cruisers fired two blasts from their laser guns. *Swoomp-swoomp!* The laser blasts whizzed by Klyk's ship as Warner banked right and then back at a hard left, tilting their axis to dodge the enemy fire.

"Missed me, missed me." Warner was getting cocky. "Never going to catch me."

"Quit hotdogging, Warner!" Tara said. "And it's 'never gonna kiss me.'"

"Gross," Warner said. "Who would want to do that?"

Warner veered down into the canyons of the mountain range. The ship bobbed and weaved around the rocky outcroppings jutting up from the bluffs.

He banked right through a curving ravine. Klyk's spaceship swiveled and turned sharply around the rocky embankments. They zipped niftily through a narrow passage deep in the canyon. The Kamilions were still right on their tail.

"Come get some!" Warner said, focusing intently on the terrain ahead of them.

"Nice moves, buddy!" Kevin yelled.

"These guys are too good," Klyk said. "You have to shake them!"

"Let me take care of this." Warner narrowed his eyes and steered through the canyon.

While Warner flew, Kevin, Tara, and TJ fired off some laser beams at the enemy spacecraft. Kevin could see the alien space cruisers dipping and dodging every shot they took. These guys *were* good.

"Here we go!" Warner steered them hard left down a narrow stretch of Rocky Mountain pass. Kevin cringed watching the tight squeeze his buddy was about to make. The spacecraft banked left, then back hard right inches away from scraping the sides of the zigzagging ravine. He thought for sure they were going to crash into the mountain. But at the last second, Warner steered the

plane back and leveled them out smoothly.

"Good luck with that one, fellas!" Warner said. They all watched as one of the reptilian cruisers burst into flames trying to make the exact same turn.

Kevin looked in the monitor and zoomed in with the controls. The Kamilion had jumped out of his pod cruiser and was stranded on the side of the mountain, shaking his fist at them as they zipped off.

"Did we lose both of them?" Klyk asked.

"I only saw one of them crash!" Kevin said.

THUNK! Klyk's spaceship shook as the remaining cruiser fired something that latched onto their force field.

"What's that thing?" TJ yelled.

"Not good," Klyk shouted. "That's a pulsatron. It's going to disable our force field!"

"Well, get it off then!" Tara shouted.

"Too late," Klyk said.

ZOOMPH! The pulsatron unleashed a burst of energy that rocked the entire ship. Warner jerked in the pilot seat, and his hand skimmed across the steering sphere. The spaceship spun in the air, whipping around like an out-of-control merry-go-round.

"Warner, look out!" Kevin yelled as they careened off course toward the mountainside. The edge of their ship scraped the rocky bluff.

Kevin could hear the force field die all around them, leaving them wide open for attack. The Kamilion cruiser opened fire, barraging the ship with a vicious onslaught from its laser cannons.

"Yo!" Warner screamed at the top of his lungs. "Whoa! Little help, please!"

"Hit the invisibility shield!" Klyk shouted, but Warner was too busy swerving away from the photon blasts screaming through the air.

Kevin scanned his monitor, but he had no visual on the reptilian space cruiser. Behind him, TJ was going berserk at his firing station trying to line up the Kamilion target in his crosshairs. *Clack-clack-clack-clack clack!* TJ fired off round after round from the laser cannon.

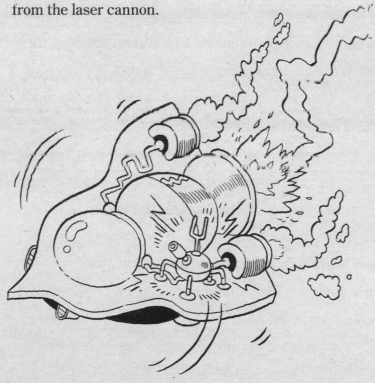

A laser blast clipped the cruiser's left wing, and the Kamilion swerved hard to the right. They all watched on TJ's screen as the cruiser crash-landed into a craggy mountain bluff.

"Got him!" TJ yelled. "Woo-hoo!"

Tara high-fived TJ while Kevin breathed a sigh of relief.

"Nicely done," Klyk said. "There may be hope for you earthlings yet."

About ten minutes later, Warner lowered them down over Max Greyson's house and hit the switch to conceal the spaceship from sight. The exit hatch opened up with a mechanical hiss. The five of them dropped down on the lawn. Tara, Warner, and TJ were all congratulating each other, slapping each other on the back and high-fiving.

They stood before a squat one-story ranch house in the boondocks of Denver. The streets stretched endlessly into the Colorado flatlands, and a never-ending line of telephone poles ran to infinity. In the distance, the Rocky Mountains peaked off the horizon.

"I must say I'm rather impressed," Klyk said,

hopping down out of the hatch. "I haven't seen flying like that since the Andromeda Riots of 1000101."

"Dude, we gotta sit down and talk sometime," TJ said to Klyk. "You must have some crazy stories."

"Yeah, maybe you could sell them to Max Greyson for his next book," said Warner.

Meanwhile, Kevin was checking the street sign and the house number against the envelope Marcy had given them.

This was the right place, but something was bugging him. Kevin scratched his head while his friends celebrated behind him.

"Kevin, what's up, man?" Warner asked as Kevin turned away from the house and walked toward Klyk's spaceship.

"I don't know," Kevin said. "Something's not adding up. How could they have caught up to us so fast or known where we were going?"

"Maybe they scanned Marcy's memory once they had her brainwashed?" Tara asked.

"They didn't have time for all that," Kevin said. "It must have been something else." Kevin walked over and inspected the wing of the ship. And there it was, right where Zouric had been thrown off. A foreign

object looked as though it was floating in midair, stuck to the invisibility shield. It was some kind of alien gadget. Kevin plucked it up and it detached easily.

"Look at this." Kevin brought the little gizmo back to the group and showed it to Klyk. "Have you ever seen one of these?"

"It's a tracking device," Klyk told them. "Zouric must have attached it when he grabbed onto the ship."

"That's what I thought!" Kevin said, kicking the dirt in frustration. "I'm getting sick and tired of these guys outsmarting us."

Kevin squeezed the alien tracking device in his hand, smashing it to bits. "Let them try and figure out where we are now. . . ."

"Good thinking, Kev," said TJ, and knocked his shoulder with a friendly punch.

"Thanks," Kevin said. "Now let's go see if this Max guy knows anything about what's going on."

Warner led them up the

cement walkway to the front stoop. "I can't believe we're really at Max Greyson's house!" he said, and rang the doorbell.

A few moments passed before the door clacked open. A chain lock held it in place. A man in his midthirties peered out through the gap in the partly opened door. He had a scruffy beard with big flat lips and a square face that made him look like a frog. Kevin could picture a long sticky tongue shooting out of his mouth to catch flying bugs.

"Hello, sir—" Kevin began.

"What do you want?" the man asked brusquely, cutting him off.

"Are you Max Greyson?" Warner asked, his voice filled with anticipation.

"It depends on who's asking," the man said.

"Why would it depend on that?" Tara asked skeptically.

The man shot her an unpleasant look. "Because I said it does."

"I think what she means is you're either him or not him," TJ said. "Regardless of whom you're talking to."

"You have about five seconds before I go take my nap." The man seemed irritated, already tired of the conversation.

"Mr. Greyson, or whoever you are, we're in big trouble and it has something to do with your comic books. We really need your help . . . please."

The door slammed shut and Kevin flinched away. "Well, I guess that's that. What now?"

But then the chain lock clinked and clattered against the door frame inside and the door swung open fully. The man stepped out onto the front stoop. He was wearing a pair of baggy sweatpants, leather sandals, and a

threadbare T-shirt with an ancient yellow mustard stain smeared across the logo of some rock-and-roll band. "I'm not Max Greyson," he said. "I'm Bjorn. Bjorn Jensen. Come inside and I can tell you what I know about Max."

Bjorn ushered them through the door, looking suspiciously up and down his deserted street before shutting the door behind them.

Kevin and his friends entered the house and were struck immediately with a thick, pungent stench that smelled like rancid food garbage. The interior of the house looked like a trash heap. Massive piles of knick-knacks and random junk filled nearly every room to the brim. Trampled newspapers cut narrow pathways through the mounds of accumulated clutter.

"Ick," Tara said, plugging her nose. "What's that smell?"

"What smell?" Bjorn asked obliviously.

TJ pulled his T-shirt over his mouth to stifle the rank odor.

"I wasn't exactly expecting company," Bjorn said, getting a little defensive.

"Sorry, Bjorn," Kevin said. "We're not trying to insult you. We just really need to talk to you about Max Greyson."

"You do know him, don't you?" Tara asked.

"Of course I know him," said Bjorn. "I used to be his assistant."

"What do you mean 'used to be'?" Warner asked. "Maybe it would be better if we got to talk to Max directly. Is he going to be home anytime soon?"

"I'm afraid I've been wondering that exact same

thing for about a year and a half. You see, Max disappeared under some very mysterious circumstances. He was mixed up in something serious."

"Wait a minute," Warner said. "Max Greyson comes out with a new comic like every three or four months. How does he do that if he's been gone for over a year?"

Bjorn explained. "Max's comics have continued to be delivered even after his disappearance. I can show you. I don't know where he is or who took him. One day he was just gone. I know it sounds crazy, but I'm pretty sure he was abducted by aliens. But I'm not supposed to talk about that. Every time I start talking about it, it just seems so unreasonable."

"You'd be surprised how reasonable it sounds to us," said Kevin. Kevin felt Klyk crawl from the top of the backpack to stand on his collarbone.

Klyk addressed the inhabitant of the house. "Max wouldn't be the first human to be abducted. Aliens are real, Bjorn, but I think you already know that. These youngsters have accidentally invited some really nasty aliens to your home planet. We need you to tell us everything you know about your friend Max."

"Whoa!" Bjorn said. "Sorry, there's a little alien talking to me. . . . It's kinda freaky!" Bjorn led them down a narrow, junk-filled hallway and opened the door at the far end. "Every few months a new manuscript for the *Brainstorm* series shows up. I take it to the publisher and keep up with the contracts and yada yada yada. It's a lot to keep track of and as you can see, I'm not the most organized person in the universe. Here's his office."

The kids along with Klyk walked in behind Bjorn and took a look around. Except for the desk, Max's office was just as cluttered with Bjorn's hoard: cardboard boxes filled with all sorts of papers; milk crates packed with old computer chargers, extension cords, and jumper cables; a mountain of vintage board games and *Star Wars* action figures on the futon against the wall; and at least three or four filthy microwaves stashed among the squalor, which gave the place a stale reek of old buttered popcorn.

Bjorn reached into an open desk drawer and took out a strange-looking object. It was about the size of a billiard ball and had seven different metal rods with rounded bulbous tips sprouting out of it.

"This thing was all that was left behind after Max was abducted," he said. "Every time one of Max's manuscripts appears, this thing lights up like the Fourth of July."

"Have you gotten the latest edition?" Warner asked.

"Oh, yeah," he said. "It's one of the best in years. Two of the biggest, baddest aliens land on Earth and start brainwashing the entire human race. They've got it all. Brain-wiping capability. Impulse-control technology. Total neural override. They even have these crazy nanobugs that fly around and inject people in their brain stems with microscopic mind control."

The freshly transmitted proofs for the latest edition of *Brainstorm* were spread out on the desktop.

"Zouric and Nuzz . . . ," Kevin said under his breath.

"That's correct," Bjorn replied, looking at him quizzically. "But how did you know that?"

"Those bad guys aren't make-believe," Warner said. "They're the real deal, and they've just taken over Oregon and pretty soon the entire planet!"

"Dang," Bjorn said, scratching his head. "That's pretty heavy, man." He gathered the transmitted proofs of the comic and handed them over for Klyk and the kids to examine. "This one just came back for review

from the publisher. It'll hit stores in the next couple of days."

"Not if Zouric and Nuzz have anything to do with it," Kevin said.

"Have a look. Take your time," Bjorn said. "See what you can find."

The kids poured over the latest edition of Max Greyson's *Brainstorm*.

The first page illustrated Zouric and Nuzz experimenting with the blue alien nanojuice to work as a mind-control serum. But they needed a delivery system, so Nuzz developed the robotic insects to unleash their diabolical plague. The panels on the third page depicted

their secret weapon in action as they released the swarm on the Kamilions, and showed Nuzz controlling the insects and the brainwash victims with a high-tech computer system aboard their ship. The reptilian warrior race didn't even know what hit them. Before they knew it they were a mindless slave army for Zouric and Nuzz.

"So the only reason Zouric and Nuzz have an army at all is because of these mind-control robot bugs, right?" said Kevin.

"They must be receiving the signal from Zouric and Nuzz's mother ship," TJ added.

"Then all we have to do is get onto the ship and jam up the signal," Tara said.

"Wait . . . that actually sounds kind of hard," TJ said.

"Hey, check this out." Warner said, flipping to the final page. "It's a blueprint of Zouric and Nuzz's mother ship!"

Kevin examined the map of the spacecraft. "It looks like they can operate the wireless mind-control mechanism from here. . . ." He pointed to a room next to the mainframe at the center of the mother ship.

"Then that's what we have to do," Warner said. "Go back to camp and figure out a way to jam their network."

"It's the only way," Klyk agreed. "We have to go back and stop them once and for all."

"You guys leaving so soon?" Bjorn asked. "But you only just got here!"

Warner shrugged. "Time flies when you're saving the world from alien psychopaths."

"Oh, but please, at least let me get you something to eat," he insisted. "I—I don't get visitors too often."

Kevin's stomach grumbled a little at the mention of food. "I am kind of hungry," he said. "We did miss breakfast."

"Then it's settled." Bjorn clapped his hands in excitement. "You can't save the world on an empty stomach, now can you?"

"Whatcha got?" Warner asked.

"Couple boxes of Pop-Tarts, box of granola bars, pomegranate juice," Bjorn said, listing the menu. "That's about it."

"Sounds good to us," Kevin said. "We're not too picky."

Bjorn jogged off to the kitchen to prepare the breakfast, even though it was after lunchtime by now. "Coming right up!"

"Nice guy," said TJ. "Kinda weird though. . . ."

DING! Bjorn's toaster sprang up two piping-hot Pop-Tarts.

Kevin, Warner, Tara, and TJ sat around the kitchen table while Bjorn kept the Pop-Tarts coming. The never-ending junk pile wasn't quite as bad in the kitchen, although Kevin was pretty sure he saw at least three dead cockroaches by the wastebasket next to the fridge, information he thought best to keep to himself before chow time. At the center of the table, Klyk paced back

and forth with his arms clasped behind his back. "The nanobots must be tapped into the ship's mainframe wirelessly."

"I was thinking the same thing," TJ said, chewing a mouthful of granola bar.

"Excuse me, everybody," Bjorn said, flopping two more Pop-Tarts onto a half clean serving plate. "I'll be right back. I think I have some more Pop-Tarts in the pantry."

Kevin glanced at the clock. "Okay, you guys," he said. "Bjorn's cool and all, but we gotta finish up and get out of here."

"Yo, Bjorn," Tara yelled across the kitchen. "Never mind, we're good on the Pop-Tarts."

Bjorn did not respond.

Kevin stood up from his seat at the breakfast table. "Bjorn?" he called. Kevin snatched Klyk off the middle of the table and propped the little cyborg on his

shoulder. He then walked into the pantry, his friends following quickly behind them.

"What is it, Kev?" Warner asked.

A warm summer breeze drifted inside the pantry through a cracked-open window. At their feet, a box of Pop-Tarts lay on the black-and-white-checkered floor, spewing out two aluminum foil packages of the breakfast pastry. Stacks of smelly old pizza boxes covered the rest of the floor.

"He's not here," Kevin said. "Where the heck did he go?"

A familiar mechanical whir buzzed overhead. The kids looked up to see one of the fluttering alien nanowasps about to attack.

The robo-bug circled the air near the ceiling and swooped down in a spiral.

"Watch out!" TJ yelled, flailing his arm and trying to backhand the mechanical pest.

In a flash, Klyk aimed his mini photon blaster at the flying robot insect and fired, zapping both its wings off and sending it crashing to the floor.

Kevin closed the pantry window and peered out through the smudged, dirt-caked pane of glass. A dark cloud of alien mind-control insects swept across the

Colorado mountainside.

"Where the heck is Bjorn?" Warner shouted.

"I don't know!" Kevin yelled over the ambient buzzing growing louder and louder every second they hesitated.

Quickly, the kids bolted out of the pantry. "Bjo-orn!" they all called as they ran around the house, wading through heaps of trash, trying to shut all the doors and close every window.

Kevin hustled out of the living room and into the entrance hall. His three friends halted next to him near the front of the house. Bjorn stood by the front door with his hand on the knob, ready to fling the thing open wide and let in the swarm.

Kevin gasped as Bjorn craned his neck back at them. It looked like someone had stuffed two lumps of coal in his eye sockets, and Kevin could see the signature mind-control puncture wound on the back of Bjorn's neck.

"One of those stingamabob things already got him!" Tara cried.

Bjorn's mouth opened and closed as if he were talking, but the voice coming from his vocal cords was surely not his. "Now the time has come—Kevin Brewer, Warner Reed, Tara Swift, and TJ Boyd—to pay for your transgressions against the grand conqueror!"

Bjorn flung the main door wide open with a flourish, and a swarm of nanowasps surged into the house, swirling in a corkscrew.

"Retreat!" Kevin shouted. They all doubled back down the scrap-cluttered hallway toward Max's office.

The swarm of nanowasps pecked at the air behind them. Kevin ran helter-skelter to the opposite side of the house behind his three friends.

Klyk rode on Kevin's clavicle, clutching his earlobe

for balance. The mini alien pulled out his tiny ray gun and started blasting the airborne alien buggers.

ZAP! Klyk nailed one of the nanowasps getting a little too close and the mechanical bug dropped to the ground. *ZAP! ZAP!* Two more alien robo-wasps bit the dust. *ZAP!* A fourth one caught the full complement of Klyk's ray gun's blast.

The four of them hit the brakes in front of the door to the home office. They all ran in and slammed the door shut behind them as the cloud of alien insects bombarded the office door from the hallway.

Kevin locked the office from the inside as the barrage of robo-bugs slammed against the door like a hailstorm pelting a tin rooftop.

A loud thud pounded outside in the hallway as Bjorn threw his weight against the door. "Open up, earthling scum, and pay for your crimes against the grand conqueror!"

"No way, dude," Warner shouted. "Tell the grand conqueror we don't want to be a part of his psycho club."

Bam! Bam! The door shuddered as Bjorn continued to bang and shout, jiggling the lock vigorously, and the alien insects burrowed and squirmed under the crack at the base of the door. One of the little alien buggers wormed its way through the keyhole and launched itself triumphantly in the air.

ZAP! Klyk blasted the nanobug and watched it fall to the floorboards.

Tara quickly shoved a piece of bubble gum in her mouth and chewed it up and stuck it in the keyhole.

Kevin broke off from the group and ran over to the window. A black iron security grate made it impossible

to escape. "You guys!" he shouted over Bjorn's pounding outside the office. "There's no way out of here."

Crunch-splat, crunch-splat! TJ stomped desperately at the alien robo-bugs crawling under the door. The neon blue nanofluid oozed out in a thick puddle beneath the soles of TJ's sneakers.

"We have to seal them out!" Warner said, dashing from the closet to the door. He carried over a box of winter clothing filled with hats, mittens, and scarves. Placing the box on the floor, Warner dropped to his knees and started stuffing the wool garments under the door until no more nanobugs were able to squeeze through.

Oddly, Bjorn had stopped trying to bust the door down. All Kevin could hear now was the buzzing of the alien insects, flapping their metal wings.

He turned around to see TJ crushing the last of the alien insects still in the room. "Maybe we shouldn't be smashing them like that, TJ," Tara said.

"Why not?" he asked. "They're trying to sting us and turn us into Nuzz's mind slaves."

"That's why," she said, pointing at TJ's feet.

The blue nanovenom was crawling up TJ's sneakers, curling around his ankles, and beginning to coil around his calf muscles.

"Yuck!" TJ screamed. "Get it off me!" He kicked off his shoes and socks, but the blue alien goo was stuck fast to his skin.

Kevin quickly grabbed a pair of mittens from the box and put them on. He kneeled down and wiped the stuff off his friend's legs before cramming the mittens under the crack at the base of the door. The blue puddle on the floor spread out across the hardwood, inching toward them, and they all backed away.

"We've got serious problems," Kevin said. "The only way out of here is through that door."

"But, Kev," said TJ, raising a worried eyebrow. "Those nanobugs are out there!"

"I know that, TJ," Kevin said. "Let me know if you have another idea."

"I have an idea," said Tara, scanning the cluttered interior of the office. "Those alien robot bugs are made of metal, right?"

"So?" Warner said. "What does that have to do with anything?"

"Well, if we had a big magnet, we could catch them, you know, like with flypaper."

"Where are we supposed to get a big magnet when we're stuck in here?" Warner asked.

"I don't know." Tara shrugged. "I didn't say it was a good idea."

"Wait a second," Kevin said. "Maybe we don't have a big magnet, but what if we had a lot of little magnets?"

"Okay." Warner rolled his eyes. "I'll just go down to the magnet store and pick some up."

"Quit being such a party pooper," TJ said, rummaging through the hoard of random stuff piled around the office. "We can make our own magnets. All we need is some wire and something metal, a battery, and some tape to make an electromagnet."

"That just might work."

"There's bound to be something we can use in this trash heap!"

A sharp crack like breaking wood sounded from the doorjamb. They all jerked their heads to look at the door. Bjorn was back, this time working at the lock with a crowbar.

Without another word, the five of them sprang into action and began sifting through Bjorn's junk piles, looking for the necessary supplies. A few minutes later, they had found everything they needed: a large spool of copper wire, a new pack of extra-long nails, a box of screws, a roll of duct tape, and a whole bunch of batteries.

"All right, guys," Kevin said, cracking his knuckles and sitting on the floor. "Let's get to work."

Kevin and his friends gathered around the supplies

while the nanobugs buzzed behind the door and Bjorn scraped away at the lock. Tara sat on the other side of the room working with a screwdriver to take apart the old microwaves stacked in the corner.

"What are you doing over there, Tara?" Kevin asked

"I'm making a stronger magnet is what I'm doing. . . . Argh!" Tara pulled the plastic panel off one of the microwave ovens and unscrewed the transformer from the old kitchen appliance. "These microwave transformers can generate a higher magnetic field than those nails." Kevin never would've thought of that but he could see where she was going. While Tara took apart the other microwaves, the boys finished their smaller electromagnets, using up every last bit of the supplies.

In just a few minutes the boys had made about two dozen electromagnets. "Good job, fellas!" Kevin said. "Now let's figure out some way to hang them in front of the doorway."

The door creaked dangerously close to popping open as Bjorn pried away with the crowbar, trying to crack the lock.

"Tara, are you almost done?" Kevin asked.

"Just a couple more minutes," she said, clipping three sets of jumper cables to a battery pack that was connected to the microwave transformer.

"We don't have a couple minutes!" Warner shouted. "Bjorn's going berserk out there."

"I'm going as fast as I can," she said.

As Tara finished making three super-strong electromagnets, Kevin and the guys knotted their own

homemade
magnets
with string
and hung
them in front
of the doorway
like birthday party
streamers.

"Okay, all finished!" Tara shouted. "Now let's test these puppies out!" She lifted one of the flat metal transformers and aimed it at a metal screwdriver. The screwdriver levitated off the ground and latched onto the supercharged electromagnet. She picked up one and ordered Kevin and TJ to pick up the other two. "We'll use them like shields." Over by the door, a few of the robo-bugs squeezed through the cracked wood and flew into the office.

The nanobugs whizzed through the booby-trapped doorway. *Thwack-thwack-thwack!* The first wave of nanobugs clanked into the homemade electromagnets dangling in their flight path and stuck, unable to break

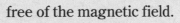

free of the magnetic field.

"It's working!" Kevin shouted, and then he remembered. At the last second, he doubled back and ran over to Max's desk.

"Kevin, what are you doing?" TJ hollered.

"The transmitter!" Kevin yelled. He snatched the transmitter Bjorn had shown them off the desktop and tossed it in his backpack along with the comic book blueprint of the mother ship.

Crack! Bjorn's crowbar shot through the wooden doorjamb and the lock popped clean off. The door swung open with a bang and the swarm of robotic insects flew into the electromagnetic booby-traps.

"Now!" Tara yelled.

Warner dropped his shoulder into Bjorn's belly and the big brainwashed lug fell back into a pile of his own rubbish.

Kevin took off running after his friends, holding the microwave electromagnet in front of his face to shield him from the swarm. The flying metal nanobugs clinked and clanked as the supermagnets pulled them out of the air.

As he booked down the hallway, Kevin felt one of the nanowasps land on the side of his neck. Its pointy metal feet clung to the skin beneath his earlobe. Kevin was about to scream and try to shake the bug off, but then two zaps from Klyk's mini ray gun struck the robotic insect.

"Thanks, man!" Kevin said to his alien pal as the nanobug crashed to the floor.

"Don't worry, Kevin. I got your back," said Klyk, shooting down another nanobug. "Or at least the back of your neck."

Kevin raced through the swarm of nanowasps toward his three human friends, who were shooting out the front door of the house. The kids hightailed it across the lawn and quickly boarded Klyk's spaceship. Kevin closed the hatch behind them before the mechanical swarm of alien mind-control insects could reach their craft.

As they cruised back to Northwest Horizons, Kevin sat quietly trying to gather his thoughts. They knew what they had to do now, but he was getting nervous about how they'd do it and whether or not they even could.

"Hey, guys, check this out," Tara said from one of the copilot seats. She pointed to the camera screen and zoomed in. Kevin crossed the deck of the ship and looked over Tara's shoulder along with TJ.

A dark cloud mass shifted and spiraled as the alien insects swept

over the cities and neighborhoods, a million black dots swirling high above all the people they were going to infect.

"Look how many there are," TJ said.

"What's going on over there?" Warner called from the pilot seat.

"There's like a jillion of those mind-control bugs flying in a huge swarm below us," Tara said.

"Make sure those things can't detect us," Kevin suggested.

"Activate the invisibility shield," Klyk said. "We're going to be back at camp in a few minutes anyway."

Warner flicked on the high-tech

camouflage, and their spacecraft disappeared against the afternoon sky.

From their vantage point up in the air, Kevin could see the whole camp. Everything was still motionless from the freeze-ray bomb. Zouric and Nuzz's alien mother ship levitated low to the ground above the center of camp. A fleet of reptilian space cruisers floated around the mother ship. Swarm clouds of the mind-control nanowasps emerged periodically from the interior of Zouric and Nuzz's massive space vessel, flying off in various directions to infect more and more of the population with Nuzz's mind-control serum.

Kevin and his friends hovered above the pinewoods,

studying the operation, watching swarm after swarm being released from the mother ship. Except for a few random patrols, Kevin didn't see many Kamilions prowling around on guard. As they waited, Klyk called the four of them over and the kids gathered around the miniature alien.

"We can't go in there unarmed," Klyk began. "First we have to retrieve Warner's bag from the robotics lab. What weapons are in the bag?"

"The wormhole generator, the shrink ray, and the freeze ray are all out of juice," Warner listed the contents of his bag. "We still have the de-atomizer ray."

"Yeah, but we can't use it," Kevin said.

"Why not?" Warner asked.

"It'll kill them!" said TJ.

"So what?" said Warner. "They're trying to kill us!"

"We can't kill them, dude," Kevin said. "If we kill one of them, the rest will know. It's a hive mind. They'll know we're here."

"Besides, it's not their fault that they're brainwashed," Tara said. "They don't deserve to die."

"All we have to do is turn the power down," Klyk told him. "Make it nonlethal. Like a stun gun. That's the easy part. The hard part is going to be getting our hands on some power cells to charge up our weapons."

"Where are we going to get those?" Kevin asked.

"The Kamilions will definitely have extra power cells on them," said Klyk.

Tara raised an eyebrow. "How are we supposed to get them?"

"That's the tricky part." Klyk scratched his alien noggin.

Kevin turned to TJ, who was sitting cross-legged on the spaceship floor, looking through his backpack. TJ pulled out the roll of duct tape from Max Greyson's office and then scrounged up a small handful of spare change from the bottom of the bag.

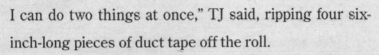

"Dude, are you even listening?" Warner said.

"Yes. Unlike some people, I can do two things at once," TJ said, ripping four six-inch-long pieces of duct tape off the roll.

"So, what's the other thing you're doing besides not listening?" Tara asked.

"I'm making us armor," TJ said, holding up a gray strip of tape with six nickels stuck to the center. "For the backs of our necks."

"Good thinking, man!" Kevin said excitedly.

"I want one!" Warner exclaimed.

"I want three!" Tara said.

"There's only enough for four," TJ said as he finished pressing the metal coins into the sticky side of the tape. "That means one each."

Kevin slapped the makeshift armor on the back of his neck and smashed it hard against his skin. No way those little nanowasps were going to sting them now. Since the alien buggers only targeted the back of the neck, this covering would work well. And their stingers would never get through the coins. Everyone else followed suit and they were ready for phase one: get their gear back.

Warner steered their unseen spaceship away from

camp and docked low to the ground on the outskirts.

Kevin, Warner, Tara, TJ, and Klyk dropped down from the spacecraft and scuttled into the underbrush. They were on their hands and knees, camouflaged by the dense thicket in the woods.

Kevin's stomach churned as they snuck through the cover of the freeze-ray-bombed forest and edged up the main dirt road. Their once-beloved science camp was now enemy territory. He had no idea if they could actually pull this off. Stealing power cells and snagging their backpack was one thing. But sneaking onto an enemy spacecraft filled with giant alien reptiles and two of the most dangerous space criminals in the galaxy to jam up their mind-control network? That wasn't going to be any kind of picnic. If they failed, it would be the end of the human race. And Kevin and his friends would be to blame. The very notion made him sick. He pushed the bad thoughts out of his mind and focused on the mission. All they could do now was try to make things right again.

"Kev, you okay, man?" Warner asked. "We ready to do this?"

Kevin nodded. "Ready as we'll ever be."

They lurked cautiously through their freeze-rayed counselors and fellow campers. Head Counselor Dimpus had his hands cupped around his mouth, still trying to shout instructions. Little Bobby Little, who nearly had been eaten by Poobah, Mim's pet arachnopod, earlier that same morning, was frozen in a running stance with one knee up and both arms pumping, making a break for the camp vans. Alexander stood with his hands blocking his face from when Nuzz had refreezed him after questioning. A dark spot still marked the pee stain on his pant leg. Everyone was trapped in awkward, chaotic poses, caught in the middle of trying to flee the alien invasion.

Beyond their freeze-rayed friends, a duo of
Kamilion henchmen strutted through camp on security detail with their laser rifles strapped over their
shoulders.

Kevin looked over at his friends and mouthed the
words: *Don't move* . . .

Kevin, Warner, Tara, and TJ all froze, mimicking
the frantic poses of everyone else around them.

The two alien henchmen sauntered past the
kids, who were hidden amid the field of freeze-rayed
campers.

Tara's eyes bugged out of their sockets as she tried to stop herself from hyperventilating. TJ closed his eyes and froze in place next to Warner, who was beside Alexander's freeze-rayed figure.

One of the lizard beasts gibbered something to his partner, and the other one yawped something back, speaking in their alien language.

The giant humanoid lizard moved toward Kevin and his friends, scanning the freeze-rayed campers. It looked like the Kamilions were going to move on when one of them stopped and sniffed the air.

Shoot, Kevin thought, his blood pressure rising. Dirty laundry! He took a subtle whiff of his armpit and made a sour face. Man, he stank! How many days had it been since he showered? He tried to remember. Obviously, it had been way too long.

They all watched as the reptilians looked around suspiciously. The Kamilions snapped their tongues out into the air. Kevin watched the alien lizard tongues extend out and recalled from his science class that some reptiles have two olfactory systems. They can smell with their nostrils and also with their tongues.

Kevin's stomach rumbled audibly as the alien reptiles walked off, continuing their patrol down by the lakeside.

"Do you see those silver canisters strapped to their belts?" Klyk asked the four of them as they stretched and breathed deeply after their freeze. Kevin could see the cartridges glistening in the daylight. "Those are the power cells we need to charge up our weapons. . . ."

There was no way they could grab the cartridges now. First they had to get back to the robotics lab for Warner's backpack. They snuck through the last of the freeze-rayed campers and hurried across the grounds to the lab trailer on the other side of camp.

Kevin, Warner, Tara, and TJ ducked around the corner of the trailer and paused for a second. "Where's

Klyk?" Tara whispered.

Kevin looked back behind them and saw Klyk hustling toward them.

"Come on, man," Kevin whispered as loudly as he dared. "Hurry up!"

Out of nowhere, a lime green light flashed brightly. The kids watched in horror as Klyk was suddenly frozen in some inescapable bubble of plasma.

They watched in silence while another one of Zouric and Nuzz's brainwashed henchmen came into view. Only this one wasn't Kamilion. She was human and armed with a freeze ray.

Marcy walked over robotically and picked Klyk off the ground. Kevin immediately felt sick. Their loyal friend Klyk was now Zouric and Nuzz's prisoner. What were they going to do? This mission was already going to be next to impossible, and without Klyk by their side, the fate of the world seemed more uncertain than ever. Kevin didn't know what to do, or whether he would ever see his friend again.

Marcy paused for a long moment before walking off

with Klyk back toward the mother ship.

Marcy gazed up at the massive spacecraft, and her eyes began to glow. A thin laser beam extended from the doorway of the ship and blinked as it scanned Marcy's eyeballs.

A few seconds later, the ramp descended automatically and the brainwashed soccer camper carried Klyk on board the spaceship.

"Klyk . . ." TJ's eyes widened and started to well up a little.

Kevin couldn't believe it. His heart sank into his stomach. But he had to be strong and keep pushing on with their plan.

"What are we going to do?" Tara asked. "We have to rescue him."

"We will," Kevin said with as much confidence as he could muster.

"But first we have to stick to the original plan," Warner said. He ducked into the robotics lab and came back out quickly with his backpack slung over one shoulder.

Kevin rustled through the bag of gear and pulled out the de-atomizer ray.

Kevin fiddled with the buttons on the side of the handheld death ray. Just as Klyk had said, he lowered the power level on the de-atomizer to make it non-lethal.

"Now what?" Tara asked.

"Time to go hunting," Kevin said. "We have to find some reptilians and take them out so we can get their power cells to charge up the rest of our weapons."

With that, they followed Kevin into the forest and positioned themselves along the side of the walking path. "Those two Kamilions were heading down toward the lake a few minutes ago. Their patrol should bring them back around this way any minute."

The seconds ticked by slowly while they waited. The whole area was dead silent except for the hum of the mother ship and the occasional buzz of a nano-swarm flying off to infect the population with Nuzz's mind-control technology.

Kevin's eyes picked up some movement around the bend. A couple of seconds later, two shadowlike figures strolled toward them.

Kevin peered over the freeze-rayed bush and aimed the de-atomizer ray at the henchmen. *ZIP! ZAP!*

He fired two perfect shots that struck both of them directly in the chest. The giant reptilians jolted with the shock of the blast and fell to the ground, stunned by the de-atomizer ray.

"Nice shot, Kevin!" Warner said.

Without missing a beat, they all hurried over to the two unconscious Kamilions and snatched the power cells Klyk had pointed out to them. Kevin picked up two smooth steel canisters off a Kamilion's utility belt. He dumped out the contents into the palm of his hand. Five circular metal objects that looked like oversized lithium batteries fell out and flashed in the sunlight.

"Everyone grab one and charge up!" Kevin said.

TJ pulled out the shrink ray they had miniaturized Klyk with the night before and changed the power cells. The new power cell fit perfectly and the high-tech device whirred and thrummed to life. They charged the rest of their alien defense weaponry and loaded the extra power cells into the bag.

"Okay, here's the plan," Kevin said, holding his freeze ray. "We get onto the mother ship, rescue Klyk, and jam the mind-control mainframe."

"Kevin," Tara said, her voice a little shaky. "I'm scared."

"I know, Tara," Kevin whispered firmly. "Me too. But we're the only thing preventing these alien freaks from taking over our planet. Now let's go in there and show them what happens when you mess with Northwest Horizons Science Camp!"

"How are we supposed to get on board?" TJ asked. "They have to scan your eyeballs before you can get on."

Kevin thought for a moment and then gestured toward the unconscious reptilians on the ground in front of them.

Now fully equipped, the four science campers dragged and lugged one of the zapped-out Kamilions across the campgrounds.

They propped the alien reptile up and opened its eyelids toward the eyeball scanner. The ship's security laser flashed and dazzled over the reptilian's eyeballs.

The access ramp opened.

They stepped into the belly of the alien mother ship.

Kevin swallowed hard as the entrance closed swiftly behind them.

Game on.

The interior of the spaceship had a wet, moldy stink—like the reptile house at the zoo. The hallway walls curved like a tunnel. Identical corridors of gray, bolted metal led to the left, to the right, and straight on ahead.

"Be careful, guys," Tara said, slipping on the newly charged positron force field gloves. "Kamilions could be around every corner."

Kevin stopped for a moment and looked at the blueprint of the mother ship from the latest *Brainstorm* comic book. He dragged his finger along the map of the ship. "If we go straight, it looks like we'll hit the prison block, where they keep their captives. Klyk should be in there. . . ."

He clasped the freshly charged freeze ray in his hand.

Kevin's shoulder felt light. In just a short while he had grown so used to Klyk perched on his collarbone that for a moment he almost forgot the little guy wasn't there. *Don't worry, Klyk,* he thought. *We're gonna find you and then you and I will take down these extraterrestrial jerks once and for all.*

They moved through the alien mother ship, holding their weapons two-handed in front of their face and

then pointing them purposefully around every corner like cops in a movie raiding a suspect's house.

Warner had the wormhole generator strapped to his forearm. Tara held her hands up wearing the positron force field gloves. They stood back-to-back. Kevin held the freeze ray and entered the next corridor after them. TJ came in last, walking backward, covering them from behind with the shrink ray.

As they stood in the middle of the hallway, a mechanical cranking sound exploded around them.

Thick steel doors at either end of the hallway began to lower, sealing them inside. "Dude, use the freeze ray!" Warner shouted.

"On what?" Kevin yelled.

"On the doors, dummy!" Tara screamed.

Kevin spun around and zapped all three doors, which stopped them from closing about two feet off the ground.

Kevin could hear a dull hum coming from the ends of the hallway. "Uh-oh . . ."

"It's getting louder," TJ observed.

The distant humming turned into the mechanical buzzing they now knew all too well. In a flash, a fleet of nanobugs flew under the gap of the door. "Unfreeze them!" Tara yelled.

Kevin blasted the freeze ray at the door at the end of the corridor and it closed all the way to the floor. But it was too late. The nanobugs had already breached the hallway. Hundreds of them zipped through the air, threatening to sting the backs of their necks.

Tara punched the air with the force field gloves, but

the swarm was too dense. The robotic insects funneled around the positron charge and landed in a large writhing mass on the back of her shirt.

"Come on, guys, we gotta get outta here!" TJ got down on all fours and retreated back under the gap of the door they had just come through. Kevin fired a freeze-ray blast at the swarm, but only three nanobugs dropped to the ground. There were far too many still flying. Kevin spun away from the swarm and slid under the door, but Warner and Tara were caught in the middle of the spaceship hallway under heavy attack from the alien nanowasps.

"EEEEK!" Tara shrieked as a dozen alien wasps climbed up her neck.

"Tara!" TJ shouted, looking under the gap at the base of the door. "Warner! Come on!"

One of the mind-control bugs landed on the nape of Tara's neck, trying to peck through the shield of coins taped there.

"Help!" Tara squealed, and Warner plucked the bug off, but not before Tara felt its stinger dangerously scrape through the duct tape and prick her neck.

Warner slammed the robotic insect to the floor with a clank.

"Warner, look out!" Kevin fired another shot of the freeze ray at the tiny flying alien bugger, but the beam of cryoplasma missed and hit the hallway wall instead. Warner whapped the back of his neck with his hand and Kevin saw the duct-taped coins fall to the floor with a clunk. Warner howled as the nanobug descended on his neck and stabbed its little stinger into Warner's brain stem. "Yowww!"

"Nooo!" Kevin yelled at the same time Tara yelped and fell to the ground, clutching her neck.

Both Warner and Tara lay collapsed in the middle of the spaceship corridor in a swirl of alien robo-bugs.

Kevin and TJ watched helplessly, knowing they had no choice but to leave their two teammates behind. There were too many nanowasps to go back and help them. Kevin flicked the controls to reverse the freeze ray and the door clanked shut, cutting off the nano-bugs from the corridor they were now in. Kevin and TJ checked each other for any nanobugs clinging to their clothes. They were both clean.

Kevin clenched his fist and punched the steel wall with all his might. A sharp pain shot through his wrist and he shook his fingers out, then kicked the wall for hurting him. "No, no, no, no, no!"

"Kevin, calm down," TJ said. "Don't hurt yourself. Everything's going to be okay!"

"Is it, TJ?" Kevin yelled, letting his emotions get the best of him. "Or are we all doomed to become slaves to that psychopathic brain alien?"

"Hey, man!" TJ said. "Snap out of it. It's up to us now. Just me and you. You're always telling us to never give up, so now's your chance to practice what you preach!"

Kevin breathed deeply and let his rational thinking take over. "You're right. We can do this," he said. "We've just got to be smarter than them, right?"

"That's right, man," said TJ.

"Only me and you now," Kevin said, calming down a little.

"Just the two of us," TJ said.

"We can do this," Kevin said, almost believing what he'd just said.

"Let's get these suckers," TJ said, balling up his fist.

"For real," said Kevin, fist bumping his pal. "Nobody messes with the Extraordinary Terrestrials!"

"Wait a minute, though," TJ said. "Don't we need a plan?"

"We've got the map. We've got the shrink ray and we have the freeze ray," Kevin said. "We've got to get you to the control room first. And while you're hacking into their network, I'm going to supersize Klyk and break him out of jail."

Kevin and TJ backtracked through the mother ship and hustled past the closed ramp entrance. Jogging side by side, they paused for a moment and glanced at the ship's blueprint, trying to figure out the best way to go. "Hang a left," Kevin said, and then folded up the map, tucking it into his back pocket. They headed through another identical corridor and turned the corner. Kevin gazed down the spaceship corridor. At the far end of the hallway, two reptilian henchmen appeared and halted at the sight of Kevin and TJ.

The two boys put on the brakes and skidded to a stop.

"This is what happens when you mess with my

science camp!" Kevin pulled out the freeze ray and fired a plasma blast that nailed one of the two Kamilions square in the chest. The alien lizard went rigid, crouched on one knee with his space laser pistol aimed at them.

Kevin fired again, but the second Kamilion dove behind his paralyzed partner. The reptilian henchman fired off two rounds of photon laser beams. The shots went low and made Kevin and TJ dance in place while the laser blasts missed their feet and scorched the floor.

"Whoa!" TJ yelped and backed up.

Kevin fired once more, but the freeze ray only struck the Kamilion who was already frozen. "He's using him as a shield," Kevin shouted to TJ. "Hit him with the shrink ray!"

TJ lifted the shrink ray, resting it in the palm of his hand. The touch screen flipped open and TJ selected his target, aiming right at the statue-still Kamilion.

Before he could shoot, two more reptilian henchmen appeared in the door frame. They opened fire on Kevin and TJ, and the boys juked and dodged the flurry of laser beams.

TJ pulled the trigger on the shrink ray and ducked away from the laser beams at the same time. The shrink-ray beam went high and missed, hitting the ceiling. The metal panel shrunk down to the size of a textbook and landed on one of the Kamilions, knocking him unconscious.

ZAP! ZAP! ZAP! The three Kamilions fired again from behind their frozen comrade.

"Retreat!" Kevin shouted. As they rushed away from the Kamilions, a barrage of photon beams zinged by their heads. Reptilian footsteps clomped after them, echoing through the steel hallways of the alien mother ship.

The two boys flew through a doorway, and Kevin stopped to look around. They were in some kind of a boiler room with a bunch of pipes and a generator. Steam wafted around the small, cramped room. All sorts of odd-looking machines blipped and bleeped.

"Dead end," Kevin said.

TJ ran out into the hallway and came right back inside as the brainwashed Kamilions rounded the corner. "Really dead end," TJ said, realizing the Kamilions had corralled them into a room with no exits.

Kevin spotted a button on the inside wall next to the door. He pressed it with the heel of his hand, and the door descended with a clank.

Kevin and TJ scanned the room. Their eyes both went toward one of the ventilation shafts near the ceiling.

Kevin pulled out the blueprint of the ship once again.

"Look here," TJ said. "This is where we are. And those air vents probably run through this whole place."

"If we pay attention," Kevin said, liking the idea, "we can get access to any room we want."

BANG! BANG! A reptilian guard pounded on the door from the hallway. Two photon blasts exploded right outside the door as the boys climbed on top of a large square machine with blinking lights. Kevin used his Swiss Army knife to unscrew the grate over the vent as the two Kamilions busted through the thick metal door.

Kevin gave TJ a boost first and got him up and in. Kevin then pushed off a valve on the wall and hoisted himself up into the vent.

"Hurry up, TJ." Kevin's voice echoed through the tinny crawl space.

The two friends slithered through the vents on their knees and elbows, shimmying their hips as they went. They were going as fast as they could, but Kevin got a knot in his chest when he heard a reptilian cackle behind them.

The Kamilion was much too big to squeeze in and give them chase, but Kevin was still right in the line of fire. The Kamilion trained his laser blaster down the vent right at Kevin's rump.

Kevin stopped crawling and turned around, aiming the freeze ray back behind him. He hit the trigger button just as the Kamilion fired his ray gun.

The plasma blast and photon beam collided—
BOOM!—right in front of the Kamilion's face.

"Growrgh!" The reptilian yowled and fell to the
ground.

Kevin whooped at the happy accident and followed
TJ through the air vent as they turned a corner, now out
of range.

TJ stopped in the claustrophobic space for a
moment. His mini pocket flashlight clicked on, and he
studied the blueprint.

He passed the map and flashlight back to Kevin and
motioned to the left, where the ventilation shaft opened
up into a room beneath it.

"This is my stop," TJ said.

The boys put their heads together to get a simultaneous view through the grate.

Through the metallic slats, Kevin peeped a bird's-eye view of the ship's control room. Two Kamilions were stationed in seats down below.

"I'll try to jam the mind-control mainframe from here. I'll trade you the shrink ray for the freeze ray," TJ whispered as they exchanged alien technology. "You're on your own until you find Klyk. Use the reverse shrink ray to supersize him, then come back here and find me. With any luck, I'll be done."

"I like the way you think," Kevin whispered back.

TJ skillfully undid the bottom screws on the grate and lifted it noiselessly.

He steadied the freeze ray on the two reptilians manning the control room.

"Wait," said TJ. "Let me see the shrink ray real quick. I don't want those big old lizard dudes frozen in my seat. . . ." Kevin handed TJ back the shrink ray.

"Make sure it's on shrink and not supersize?" Kevin asked.

"Who do you think you're dealing with?" TJ pressed the trigger button, and the shrink ray zapped one of the reptilians down to fun size. The other reptilian made a confused sound and craned his neck up to the air vent.

Zap! TJ pressed the trigger button again and shrank the second yellow-eyed lizard beast in his seat.

"Good work!" Kevin said. He took the shrink ray back from his friend and traded him the freeze ray.

"Check you on the flip side." TJ dropped down out of the vent and into the control room. He scooped up the mini reptilians and put them in a drawer before sitting down in front of the alien computer system. TJ smiled and cracked his knuckles. "Time to get to work," he said. Kevin gave his buddy a thumbs-up and pressed on through the ventilation shaft with the blueprints in hand.

Kevin shimmied a little farther down the dark air vent. He squirmed carefully through the narrow crawl space, trying not to let the extraterrestrial steel rumble with his movements. He stopped for a second and checked the blueprint. He was almost there. Up ahead,

he could see the light shining through the slats in the grate. He went toward the light and paused right above the spaceship's slammer. Rows of jail cells lined both sides of the narrow holding room.

Kevin spotted Klyk in a mini cage within one of the larger cells. He was no longer encased in the plasma, but he looked a little woozy. Locked up in the cells to the left of Klyk's were Kevin's two brainwashed friends—Warner and Tara. In the cell to the right, some kind of undulating jelly monster with tentacles was being held captive as well.

As he gazed down from the air vent, Kevin heard the door to the prison open up and listened to the clanking footsteps of Nuzz entering the room. Zouric strode in close behind it, towering over its partner.

Kevin watched silently as Zouric approached Tara's and Warner's jail cells. With one swift motion from Nuzz's robotic arm, their holding cells swung open and Tara and Warner stepped out obediently, their eyes black as night.

Kevin listened from the vent, clutching the newly charged supersizing shrink ray in his hand.

Zouric babbled something in its alien language to the freshly brainwashed minions, Warner and Tara. Kevin had no clue what any of it meant, but he knew it was probably bad news. Tara and Warner didn't seem to understand either, looking blankly at the Gastropod.

"You have to speak to them in their own language," Nuzz said to its partner. "How many times must I tell you to activate your language chip?"

Zouric tapped a button with his long slimy-looking finger and spoke again, this time in perfect English. "You will find your two other accomplices and bring

them to us unharmed. There is something I would like to do to them personally."

Kevin gulped as Zouric handed his friends back their alien weaponry—a fully charged wormhole generator and the force field gloves.

Tara pulled the gloves onto her hands and cranked up the power level. Warner had the wormhole generator in his hands and an evil glimmer in his eyes.

Tara and Warner marched out of the prison chamber to do Zouric and Nuzz's bidding. Kevin's face turned bright red with anger. All he wanted to do now was blast Zouric and Nuzz with the shrink ray, but he couldn't get a clear shot until he removed the grate from the air vent. And that would cause too much of a racket to go unnoticed. It was too risky.

Instead he watched as Nuzz went over to the gelatinous blob with the shifting tentacles. The alien brainiac reached its robotic arm through the bars of the jail cell and started petting the disgusting blob monster.

"There, there, Burbles," Nuzz said in an affectionate voice. "I don't like that you have to be down here, either. But since you can't behave yourself, this is where you'll have to stay for now."

Kevin furrowed his brow. *Is this dude really talking to that slimy alien freak beast like it's a pet?*

Kevin held his breath as Zouric and Nuzz exited the room. Klyk was alone in his mini cage.

Kevin pried off the metal grate and hopped down from the vent. He landed on the floor with a thud.

"Kevin!" Klyk's eyes lit up at the sight of his earthling pal.

Kevin made sure the alien device was set to supersize, and then aimed it at Klyk. "Say cheese!"

"Why?" Klyk asked with a look of confusion on his face.

"Because that's what you say when . . . ," Kevin started to explain. "Oh, never mind." He lined Klyk up on the touch screen pad and pushed the trigger button, but the shrink ray didn't respond.

"What the heck is wrong with this thing?" Kevin said, turning the alien device around in his hands. "It was working just fine a few minutes ago." He held the laser beam in one hand and shook it.

"Be careful with that," Klyk said, flinching away.

ZAP! The shrink ray blast skewed off to the left and struck the tentacled jelly monster in the adjacent cell.

The alien slimoeba shuddered and then expanded

to five times its normal size. Klyk, still miniaturized in his tiny cell-within-a-cell, smacked his forehead in disbelief.

The monster could now barely fit in its jail cell and was all smushed up against the prison bars. One of its now giant tentacles slithered into Klyk's cell and swept his tiny cage against the wall.

"Oomph!" Klyk groaned while Kevin lined up Klyk's cage with the shrink ray a second time.

The thing's enormous tentacle wriggled in front of Klyk's cage. "Whatever you do!" Klyk cried. "Don't hit it again!"

"I got it, I got it." Kevin took his time aiming, lining his soon-to-be-mega-sized alien friend up more carefully this time around. He waited for the tentacle to move out of the way and pulled the trigger.

Blammo!

The ray beam struck mini Klyk, and his tiny cage exploded into a thousand pieces. In a flash, Klyk grew to his normal humongous size. Kevin had almost forgotten how huge their alien ally had been once. He must

have been close to seven feet tall and roughly three hundred pounds. Klyk pulled out his full-sized ray gun and pointed it at the lock on the prison cell.

Just as Klyk was about to pull the trigger, Kevin felt a massive wet slimy thing land on his shoulder and spin him around. Before he could shoot the alien jelly monster back down to size, the thing's tentacle lifted him off the ground and Kevin found himself dangling upside down from the ceiling. The shrink ray clattered to the floor. The tentacle coiling around his left ankle tightened. The alien slime monster was moving Kevin closer and closer to its face, which was pressed between two of the prison bars.

"Help!" Kevin cried, turning to Klyk for some assistance. "It's trying to eat me!"

Nom! Nom! Nom! The slimeball slobbered and stuffed Kevin's whole foot directly into its mouth.

"Hold on, Kevin," Klyk said calmly as he cracked his neck and stretched a little bit. "I'll be right there."

The jelly monster slurped his leg a little farther, up to the kneecap.

"This is not cool, man," Kevin said.

"They should have taken my weapon away," Klyk said, ignoring Kevin as he took his sidearm out of its holster and twirled the ray gun on his finger like a cowboy. "You know one of the great things about being small? Everyone underestimates you."

"Klyk!" Kevin yelled as the jelly monster slurped Kevin's leg now up to the middle of his thigh. Kevin's leg was drenched in the alien's digestive juices, which started to sting.

Klyk blasted the lock off his jail cell with his ray gun. He strolled out and grabbed the jelly monster by the tentacle, the one holding Kevin. He twisted it hard with both hands and the thing snapped off, leaving the rest of it coiled around Kevin's ankle.

Kevin fell against the prison bars still upside down with his leg in the slimeball's mouth. Klyk picked Kevin up with both hands under his armpits and yanked back as hard as he could. Kevin felt the suction of the slime monster's throat ease up, and Kevin's leg released with a soggy pop.

Klyk stumbled back and set Kevin on the ground. "There, that wasn't so bad."

"Yeah," said Kevin. "Maybe if you're a seven-foot-tall alien cyborg cop it isn't. But I'm just a kid."

Kevin picked up the unshrink ray and dialed the settings back to shrink. He aimed it at the slimeball monster, but Klyk grabbed the weapon away from him.

"Don't waste a shot on this guy," Klyk said. "We've got bigger fish to fry. Come on."

Klyk handed the shrink ray back to Kevin, and they left the ship's prison level to go take down Zouric and Nuzz and unbrainwash their friends.

Adrenaline coursed through Kevin's entire body as he walked back to the control room of the mother ship with a full-sized Klyk at his side. He had never known anyone this strong or this powerful before, let alone ever had someone like this on his team. It felt pretty darn good. He wasn't even that scared anymore. Anybody who messed with Kevin had to get through Klyk first.

As they jogged through the maze of hallways on the spaceship, two Kamilions appeared out of nowhere. "Get down!" Klyk shouted, and nudged Kevin out of the way with a flick of his arm.

Kevin slammed into the curved steel wall, nearly

knocking the wind out of him.

PYOO! PYOO! Klyk fired two deft shots that nailed both reptilians in the abdomen and flung them unconscious to the floor.

"Whoa!" Kevin's eyes bulged. "You didn't kill them, did you?"

"They'll be out for a while," Klyk said. "But they'll survive."

Kevin clutched his abdomen and wheezed for a second but then caught his breath. A momentary surge of pride filled him up so that he didn't even have to use his inhaler.

"Be on the lookout for Tara and Warner," Klyk told him now that the coast was clear. "Zouric and Nuzz gave them orders to capture you and TJ by any means necessary."

"We have to get back to TJ," Kevin said. "He's working on the computer mainframe right now."

Kevin glanced at the map of the ship and pointed to the room where TJ was trying to jam up the mind-control technology.

"He is?" Klyk said, a little surprised. "How were you able to gain access?"

"You don't think you're the only one with a few tricks up his sleeve, do you?" Kevin said.

Pointing again at the map, Kevin whispered, "He's in this room here. Just to the left." Kevin crouched down and peered around the corner. Two reptilian henchmen stood outside, guarding the door.

"How'd you get past the guards the first time?" Klyk said.

"We didn't," Kevin said. "We took the air vents. They must not even know he's in there yet."

"You want to take the shot?" Klyk asked.

"Yeah, I got this one." Kevin peeked around the corner again and aimed the shrink ray at the Kamilions guarding the door.

The alien lizards didn't even see the shots coming. Kevin blasted both of them and they shrank down to miniatures. The mini reptilians opened fire, but their tiny laser guns did nothing as Kevin and Klyk marched

down toward the control room. They pressed the entry button, and the door opened up. Inside, TJ whipped around in his seat and trained the freeze ray on them.

"Whoa, dude." Kevin put his hands up. "Little jumpy, are you?"

"Jeez, you scared the crud out of me!" TJ said, a smile crossing his face as he looked at Klyk. "No offense, but you're way scarier when you're big."

"I thought you were supposed to be unbrainwashing these guys," Klyk said.

"Yeah, how's it going?" Kevin asked.

"Not that well, I'm afraid." TJ frowned.

"Did you try accessing the—" Kevin asked, but TJ cut him off.

"I've tried everything!" TJ said. "I think Nuzz has some pretty advanced security protocols on this system. Without his encryption key there's no way to override the mind-control mainframe."

"There's no way you can crack it?" Kevin asked.

"Like I said," TJ sighed. "I tried everything I could think of."

"Uh-oh," Klyk said.

"Yeah, I

know," TJ said. "It's a
bummer."

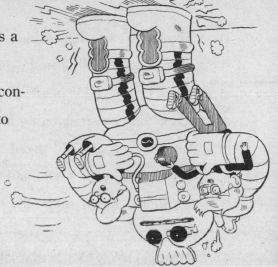

"Not the mind con-
trol." Klyk pointed to
one of the security
monitors capturing
the surveillance
camera directly
outside.

On the screen, half a dozen Kamilions were prowling down the hallway, laser pistols drawn, creeping
slowly toward the door.

"That's the only way out of here," Kevin said.

"Not the only way," TJ said, pointing toward the air
vents.

"Klyk can't fit through there," said Kevin.

TJ picked up his freeze ray and stood bravely with
his chest out. "Then we'll stand and fight!"

"Wait," said Klyk. "I have a better idea. There are no
surveillance cameras in here, so they don't know we're
in here for sure." The massive alien cyborg reached

down and flicked a switch on his robotic boots. He then scooped up Kevin and TJ under one arm and jumped straight up. Kevin felt his point of view flip upside down, and suddenly they were hanging from the ceiling.

"Antigravity boots?" TJ asked.

"Pretty cool, huh?" Klyk nodded.

"Awesome," Kevin said, adjusting the settings on the shrink ray.

"Okay, get ready," Klyk said. "Those Kamilions are gonna be coming through the door any second. And when they do, you've got to be ready to fire!"

"Here we go," TJ said.

Kevin watched the door intently, heart pounding and blood pumping quickly to his head.

The door rose up from the floor, and the three Kamilions at the front of the pack entered slowly, scoping out the room.

Klyk waited for the reptilian henchmen to let down their guard, then—*ZHOOP!* Klyk swung upside down in the door frame, hanging from the antigravity boots. The alien cyborg unleashed a barrage of ray gun blasts at the platoon of Kamilion warriors in the hallway.

Clinging tightly to Klyk, the boys dangled upside down and fired their weapons. TJ blasted three of the reptilians out in the hallway with the freeze ray.

Kevin nailed the reptilian trio inside the control room with the shrink ray.

Klyk dropped down from the ceiling with an agile flip and landed on his feet. He set the boys down right side up.

"Yeah, baby!" Kevin shouted, and gave TJ a high five.

"Those dudes didn't even see it coming!"

"Don't celebrate just yet," Klyk warned them. "Look!"

From the doorway of the control room, Kevin squinted down the corridor. The glass dome encasing Nuzz's brain glimmered in the overhead lights.

"Get him!" Kevin shouted.

Kevin, TJ, and Klyk all opened fire on one of the galaxy's two most wanted aliens. *ZAP! ZAP! PYOO! PYOO! SWOOMP!* The hallway of the spaceship lit up with the laser beams, photon blasts, and shots from the freeze ray.

But Nuzz remained unaffected—unfrozen, unshrunk, and unscathed.

"What the—" Kevin said.

"He must have some kind of force field!" TJ said.

The hologram face on the glass case protecting Nuzz's brain cackled at them evilly. Kevin looked at the mini reptilians and full-sized unconscious Kamilions on the floor around them. All the exits on the corridor clanked shut except for the one next to Nuzz.

Kevin, TJ, and Klyk raced out of the control room after Nuzz, but the maniacal alien brain-monger was already slipping away through the last open exit.

Just before he made his getaway, the mechanical alien brainiac rolled something toward Kevin, TJ, and Klyk.

Nuzz skittered out of the hallway, and the door slammed shut behind him.

Kevin watched as the metallic ball Nuzz had rolled at them stopped directly in front of them.

"We have to get out of here!" Klyk shouted frantically. "It's a fume grenade!" Their humongous alien cyborg friend squatted down in front of the locked door and lifted with all his might. The door didn't budge an inch.

In the middle of the corridor, the metallic ball opened up and let out some kind of white gas that filled the volume of the hallway.

Kevin choked and gagged on the gas. TJ coughed and sputtered. The mini reptilians passed out immediately.

Klyk tried to lift the spaceship door one more time, but it was no use.

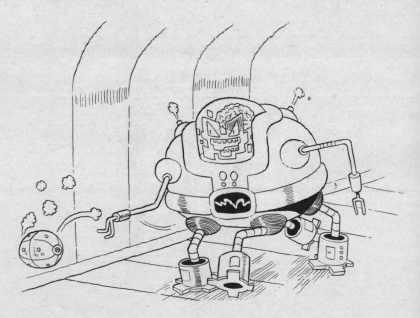

Kevin looked at Klyk helplessly with his eyebrows raised.

Klyk opened his mouth and spoke through the cloud of noxious fumes. "It's a sleep grenade," Klyk said. "We're in troub—"

Before he could finish his sentence, the big alien cyborg swooned and toppled to the ground with a thud. TJ's eyes rolled back in his head, and he crumpled into a heap of limp limbs.

Kevin's mind went blank before he even hit the floor.

Kevin's eyes popped open, and a sharp, stinging pain stunned his vision. His temples throbbed from a splitting headache. He couldn't move his feet or his arms. His wrists were shackled to a metal seat. Next to him, TJ and Klyk sat captive, restrained in prisoner seats of their own. Kevin looked around and saw they were being held in the main flight deck and operations center of Zouric and Nuzz's ship. A huge viewport window curved in a semicircle around the room above a massive control panel.

Kevin had a clear view of their frozen science camp, the forest in the distance, and the night sky up above. How long had they been knocked out for? Kevin

had no idea. The reptilian army surrounded the massive room, blocking all the exits. Mixed in with the Kamilion army, the entire girls' soccer camp trained their brainwashed gazes on Kevin, TJ, and Klyk. Marcy stood stiffly at the front of the platoon of brainwashed soccer players.

Tara and Warner stood at the front on either side of Zouric and Nuzz, the galaxy's two most wanted aliens.

"Let us go!" TJ shouted at Zouric and Nuzz.

"I'd be quiet if I were you," Klyk muttered to the boys.

"I would listen to your oversized friend," Nuzz agreed. He skittered forward on his robotic legs to get closer to his prisoners. "Resisting the inevitable will only make matters worse. And as you'll see, there's nothing any of you can do." Nuzz's robotic arm motioned to a large bank of video monitors above the control panel. On the screens, various shots from all over the western hemisphere showed cities being taken over by the mind-controlling nanobugs. "Take a look for yourselves. We've already succeeded with our mission. Within the hour, half of your planet's population will be under our control. By tomorrow morning, the entire planet will be ours. And there's nothing you can do about it." Nuzz cackled. "How does that make you feel?"

Kevin and TJ said nothing, but Kevin's stomach sank at the sight of his fellow humans being brainwashed by Nuzz's nanoserum.

Nuzz continued, addressing Kevin, "Without further ado, allow me to induct you and your friend into my army of slaves."

Kevin watched as Zouric handed two of the nanobugs to Tara. She took off one of the force field gloves and approached the boys, holding the robotic mind-control insect. The nanowasp squirmed and wriggled menacingly between her fingertips.

"Tara, it's me!" Kevin pleaded with her. "Tara, I know you're in there. Don't do this!"

"She can't hear you," Nuzz said. "She only answers to me now."

Tara stepped behind Kevin, and the nanobug buzzed loudly in his ear.

"What about me?" Klyk asked Nuzz. "What happens to me?"

"For you," said Nuzz, "Zouric and I have a much different fate in mind. You will be sent to a most unfriendly place."

"And where might that be?" Klyk asked.

"Garmonbozia," Nuzz said slowly, savoring each syllable. "You've heard of it, I'm sure. A most unpleasant place. I'm also certain you've never been there, because once you go there, you never leave."

Klyk's expression changed instantly from defiance to fear.

Zouric gestured to Warner, and Warner walked toward them. He stepped behind Klyk and held the wormhole generator to the back of his head.

"This is it," Nuzz said. "Prepare to meet your doom!"

The buzzing of the nanobug between Tara's thumb and forefinger made Kevin's head swim. He was out of ideas. How could he have let this happen? He and TJ were about to become Zouric and Nuzz's brainwashed minions along with the rest of the world.

"Well, buddy." Kevin gulped down the panic filling up in his chest. "I guess this is it. . . ."

TJ looked over at his friend. "It was nice knowing you, Kev."

"You too, TJ," Kevin said, his mind reeling. Was this really how it was going to end? "Klyk, I don't know what to say. I'm sorry I shrink-rayed you. If you had been big this whole time, we might have gotten out of this."

"You didn't know any better. No one can tell the future," Klyk said. "But from the look of it right now, our time's about to be up."

Tara moved the robotic insect closer to Kevin's neck, preparing to inject the nanovenom into Kevin's brain stem. TJ squirmed in his seat to Kevin's right as the nanobug aimed its snout at the back of Kevin's neck.

Warner clicked on the power cell of the wormhole generator and it charged up with an electric hum.

Klyk tried desperately to wrestle out of the shackles, but they were far too strong. "You'll never get away with this!" he shouted at Nuzz.

Nuzz chuckled. "We already have." The alien brainiac nodded at Tara and Warner.

Kevin winced and crinkled his brow, tensing up as he waited to be pricked.

"Get on with it," Nuzz commanded her.

But Kevin didn't feel a thing. The stinger never pierced the back of his neck.

Kevin whipped his head around just in time to see Tara spring into action. She threw the nanobug onto the ground and stamped it into a blue splotch. She slipped the force field gloves back on and lunged for Warner, grabbing him by the arm. Warner jerked back, shucking off her grip, but Tara snatched the wormhole generator off his wrist before he could blast Klyk into another dimension. With lightning-quick reflexes, Zouric and Nuzz drew their alien weaponry and fired at Tara. She dropped down on one knee as the shots from their ray guns whizzed past her head. Tara did a forward roll and came up with both hands powered up in the force field gloves.

Zouric and Nuzz fired right at her. Their aim was true, but the shots deflected off the force field and ricocheted throughout the room. Quickly she clasped the wormhole generator onto her forearm and aimed it at Nuzz.

"Freeze, sleazeball!" she shouted triumphantly.

"Tara, wait!" TJ called out from his seat. "Don't shoot him! We need him to shut down the mind-control network. He's the only one who has the encryption key!"

"I got it covered, TJ." Tara smiled. She pulled something out of her pocket that looked similar to a flash drive. "I lifted it off this lamebrain when he wasn't paying attention."

"I thought you were brainwashed!" Nuzz said to Tara.

"I was faking," Tara said, her lip curling into a devilish smirk. "The nanobugs didn't get me. The armor we

made covered the back of my neck. I just did everything that Warner did. Because he actually was brainwashed."

"Smart thinking," TJ said. "But what's the plan now?"

"I'm going to blast these two intergalactic idiots wherever they were going to send Klyk."

"You think you've won." Nuzz cackled. "But the wheels are already in motion."

"Oh, you're about to be in motion all right. Through the wormhole." She paused for a second. "Tell Morgan Freeman I said what's up."

Tara fired the generator and the wormhole twisted across the room, catching the alien mastermind in its vortex. Within a few seconds, Nuzz vanished into thin air.

Tara then pointed the generator on Zouric. "You too, buster!"

The seven-foot Gastropod yawped at the Kamilions, but Tara fired the wormhole generator once more and drilled Zouric in the chest. A moment later, Zouric disappeared, joining his partner in a very unfriendly place.

"Tara, look out!" Kevin warned as Warner leaped onto her back, trying to wrestle her to the floor. Tara steadied herself and elbowed Warner in the ribs, flinging him off her. Warner came roaring back at her and she punched at him with a force field glove, knocking him back against the wall.

Warner slumped to the floor as Tara raced over and clicked the release button to unshackle her friends. The restraints popped off and Kevin, TJ, and Klyk stood up next to Tara.

"You just knocked Warner out. That was awesome!"

TJ said, a little awestruck by what had just gone down. "I mean, not for him . . . he's probably going to have a concussion."

They looked around at the reptilian army closing in on them. The Kamilions aimed their ray guns right at the four of them, but Tara held up her force field gloves and aimed the wormhole generator threateningly at the vanguard of brainwashed reptilians. The Kamilions backed off slightly, but kept their weapons trained on the crew. Their yellow eyes burned with brainwashed fury, still under the spell of Nuzz's mind control.

Klyk spun around and raced to the nearest exit. Four Kamilions blocked their escape. He stepped up to the reptilian foursome and they lurched at the gigantic cyborg, jumping for him all at once. Klyk whirled around with a fearsome backhand that sent two of them flying across the room and slamming into the wall. The remaining two clung to Klyk, trying to drag him down, but Klyk was stronger than both of them combined. He elbowed one of them to the ground and then grabbed the fourth one by the head, whirling the man-sized reptile like a hammer and launching him into the oncoming horde.

Kevin sprinted over to the door and pushed the button to open it up. "Come on!" he shouted.

"What about Warner?" TJ yelled. Klyk raced over to their brainwashed friend. The humongous cyborg threw Warner over his shoulder, and the four of them sprinted back through the alien mother ship, leaving the soccer campers and reptilian army behind.

"This way!" Klyk shouted, and led the way back to the control room, lugging Warner's conked-out body

over his immense shoulder.

The five of them piled inside and sealed the door shut behind them. TJ sat down at the alien computer system.

Tara handed him the flash drive and he plugged it into the mainframe.

As they waited for the encryption key to activate, Kevin watched the security monitors. A tide of reptilians filled up the corridors, making their way through the spaceship toward the control room.

"Wait!" TJ said, a hint of panic in his voice. "Wait, wait, no!"

"What is it?" Kevin asked.

"It's asking for a password." TJ pointed to the screen, where a little cartoon image of Nuzz had appeared alongside a box for a password.

"What the heck would that dude's password be?" Tara asked.

Klyk pulled up Nuzz's profile on the 3D hologram. They tried his place of birth on his home planet. Then they tried

the date he became a walking, talking brain machine. But the little cartoon Nuzz icon shook his finger no at both attempts.

"I mean, I always use the name of my dog for my password," Tara said. "But I don't think Nuzz has any pets."

Kevin's eyes lit up and he looked at Klyk. "That's not true," Kevin said, leaning over the keyboard. "He's got a big slimy thing that tried to eat me." Kevin typed in the word "burbles" and hit the Return button.

The pass code registered, and the encryption key started to unlock the mind-control mainframe.

"Way to go, Kevin!" Tara cried. "You're the man, man!"

"Thanks, Tara," Kevin said. "You're the man, too. I mean, you know, the girl version."

Once the encryption code hit 100 percent, TJ tapped a few more buttons and then tapped the Return key. "Done! The nanovenom should be cut off from the wireless signal now."

Klyk sat Warner down in the seat next to TJ and

patted his face, trying to wake him up. Kevin came over by his friend and shook him, but Warner was out cold.

Up on the monitor, the Kamilions and soccer campers alike halted their march through the labyrinth of corridors. They grabbed at their heads and rubbed their eyes, disoriented and groggy.

As they came out of their brainwashed haze, Marcy and the rest of the soccer girls looked around at the giant alien lizard men surrounding them. A collective high-pitched shriek rang out through the entire mother ship. The soccer girls pushed through the Kamilions, frantically running for their lives. The reptilian army scratched their scaly heads in confusion.

WONK! WONK! WONK! WONK! Suddenly a honking sound blared throughout the alien mother ship. Red emergency lights flashed as the alarm sirens wailed.

"What's that?" Kevin asked, raising his voice over the brain-scrambling noise.

TJ made a sour face and then pointed at the screen. The monitor went black and a robotic voice came on. "Preparing for self-destruct. Count down set for one minute."

"What does that mean?" Tara asked TJ. "And why is it speaking English?"

"I reset the language before when I was trying to crack the fail-safe," he replied. "Nuzz must have created a self-destruct protocol in case anybody tries to jam the signal, including him."

"You're telling me this ship's going to blow up?" Tara said.

"If I know one thing about someone like Nuzz, it's that he's going to take us down with him. He doesn't take kindly to people messing up his plans."

"Warner, get up!" Kevin crouched down by his buddy's side and shook him a little more. "Come on, man. Get up!"

Slowly, Warner opened his eyes. He stretched his arms and yawned as if he had just woken up from a nap.

"We have to get out of here, man," Kevin told him. "This place is going to blow up!"

"What's going on?" Warner said groggily. "Where am I?"

"We're on Zouric and Nuzz's ship and it's about to blow!" Tara shouted.

Warner's eyes went wide with fear and he shot up from his seat. "What are we waiting for?"

The five of them exited the control room in a hurry and sprinted through the spaceship. But they didn't get far before they were stopped by a mass of reptilians clogging up the corridor.

The reptilians wandered around the spaceship in a daze, disoriented from the effects of the brainwashing nanoserum.

Klyk called for their attention and hurriedly explained the situation in their native alien tongue. *"Narf trumple fraw. Kip dur otch ver warf!"*

As soon as the information registered, they took

off running in a giant lizard stampede, pushing Klyk and the kids out of the way.

A robotic voice sounded over the speaker system throughout the ship. "Thirty seconds until self-destruct!"

They sprinted behind the horde of frantic Kamilions. But there were way too many of them trying to pile through the hallways of the spaceship.

"You guys!" Tara shouted. "We're never going to make it out of here in time! We need another way out!"

TJ looked at the blueprint of the mother ship. "There is no other way out!"

"Then we're just going to have to make one ourselves," Kevin said.

He led them to the outermost wall of the alien mother ship and took the freeze ray, the de-atomizer ray, and the force field gloves. He turned them up full blast and laid them on the floor of the corridor by the wall.

"These things have a ton of compressed energy," Kevin

said as the robotic voice overhead counted down past fifteen. "Klyk, let me borrow your ray gun."

Klyk handed his alien fire-arm to Kevin, who pointed it at the arrangement of alien tech-nology on the floor. "Everyone stand back," Kevin instructed his friends. He pulled the trigger and the ray gun flashed.

KABOOM!

They raced over to the smoking hole in the wall of the mother ship and looked down. The roof of one of the cabins about ten feet below made for an easy jump.

"Ten . . . nine . . . eight . . ." The self-destruct voice continued the countdown.

Klyk jumped out first and landed on the rooftop. He waited for the rest of them to jump down one by one.

"Seven . . . six . . . five . . . four . . ."

Kevin and his friends sprinted across the roof of the cabin away from the mother ship. They hung off the gutter and dropped down to the freeze-rayed grass.

"Three . . . two . . . one . . ."

Kevin plugged his ears and squinched his eyes shut tight.

Zero.

The alien mother ship exploded in the night air and crashed to the ground in the center of camp. Bright orange and blue flames spat out from the wreckage and flared out, touching the nearby evergreens. But the freeze-rayed foliage didn't burn. The mother ship slowly incinerated into a huge mass of bent and twisted alien metal.

Kevin sat there with his back to the cabin and watched the plume of jet-black smoke rise up into the starry sky. Kevin couldn't believe they had made it out. He looked over at Warner, who was lying not too far away. "Yo, man," he said. "You all good?"

"I think so," he said. "You?"

"Pretty sure . . ."

As the boys dusted themselves off and stood up out of the rubble, Tara and TJ ran over and gave them each a big hug. "We made it!" Tara shouted.

"Way to go, Kev," TJ said. "Wasn't sure we were going to get out of that one."

"What about the rest of the Kamilions?" Kevin asked.

"I think they all made it out, too!" Tara told him.

"And the soccer camp girls are all safe?" Warner asked.

"Yeah—look!" TJ pointed to Marcy, who was walking over to them.

"Hey, guys!" Marcy said.

"Marcy!" Kevin said, standing to greet her.

"I don't know what you guys did, but the last thing I remember was running with you guys into the woods and then all of a sudden I was on that spaceship. So awesome."

Kevin chuckled. "Are the rest of your friends okay?"

"Yeah, they're good," Marcy told them. "Most of 'em took off running. Totally freaked out, you know?"

Just then, Klyk walked over with one of the Kamilions. "Everyone, I'd like to introduce you to Commander Gup. I told him what happened here today and he has something to say to you."

The reptilian commander looked at the kids and spoke a few sentences in his alien language.

"He said he's never known such bravery and courage to come out of someone so young and small. And he wants you to know that he and his species will be forever indebted to you for what you did here today."

The Kamilion commander said a few more words.

"He would also like to offer you new freeze rays and help you restore the rest of your camp."

"Thank you, sir," Kevin said. "That would be amazing."

They all watched as the commander ordered his reptilian troops to begin unfreezing their fellow campers. They unfroze Poobah first and shrunk the giant arachnopod back down to size. One of the Kamilions standing by the unconscious alien creature shouted over to Klyk and the kids.

"What'd he say?" Kevin asked.

"They want to know if they can keep Poobah as their pet," Klyk said.

"Please," TJ said. "That thing's going to haunt my dreams."

"What about Burbles?" asked Tara. "There's no way we're taking care of that thing."

"Yeah," Kevin said. "Tell them to take him too. I mean, if he's still alive."

"He's still alive all right. That blob can withstand temperatures hotter than the sun!" Klyk said, then yelled back to the two Kamilions, who nodded at them before loading the arachnopod onto their spacecraft.

As the Kamilions retrieved Nuzz's pet slime monster from the wreckage of the gigantic spaceship, Kevin's backpack started to light up like the Fourth of July.

"Whoa, dude," Warner said to Kevin. "Check it out!"

"The transmitter." Kevin reached into his backpack and pulled out

the alien device they had picked up at Max Greyson's
house.

The transmitter flashed and then suddenly zapped.
They all watched as pages appeared on the frozen turf
at their feet.

"It's a comic book!" Warner said, picking it up.

The issue was similar to the proofs they had seen
with Bjorn, but with a new addition—their tale of defeat-
ing Zouric and Nuzz. Kevin's eyes widened as he looked
at the comic book and saw illustrated versions of him and
his friends on every page. Kevin with his bright orange
hair, running away from the freeze-ray bomb. Warner
flying Klyk's spaceship through the Rocky Mountains.

Tara making super-strong electromagnets out of Bjorn's microwaves. And TJ shrinking the reptilians down to size from the air vent aboard the mother ship.

"This is, like, my number one wish coming true right now!" Warner said, flipping through the draft. "My own comic book! Starring me!"

"Starring us," Tara said, clearing her throat. "Thank you very much."

"But how did he know already?" said TJ. "This just happened."

"Kind of spooky if you ask me," Tara said.

"Max must be keeping an eye on us from wherever he is," Kevin said. "Maybe he's got a time machine."

"That would be sweet," said Warner, completely awestruck. "One thing's for sure—he's definitely using *Brainstorm* to send a mcs-sage." They continued to read the comic.

They all stopped on the last page, which read:

This edition will probably be the last *Brainstorm* comic I ever write. As you already know by now, I have been taken hostage by aliens. What you may not know is that they are evil aliens out to destroy the universe. My abductors have recently found out that I've been sending secret messages to Earth detailing exploits of the most wanted criminals. This did not please them one bit. They would have killed me if they didn't need me alive. But I don't have long. Please help me. The universe is in grave danger.

"There's no way we're going to let those aliens win," Warner said.

"Not if we have anything to say about it," Kevin said.

"And we totally do," Tara said.

"We do?" TJ asked meekly. "I mean, yeah we do!

Nobody messes with the Extraordinary Terrestrials!"

Klyk smiled for the first time since the kids had met him. "Looks like you're coming to outer space."

Kevin looked up at the sky twinkling with millions of stars, thousands of planets, hundreds of alien civilizations. He was completely exhausted, but he couldn't help feeling excited at the adventure ahead. *We are really going to outer space*, he thought. His mind fluttered with the possibilities.

Before long, the Kamilions had finished unfreezing the entire camp.

The leaves blew with the breeze and the animals scampered through the forest once again. More important, all the campers and counselors were back to their usual selves, including one in particular.

Alexander marched over to Kevin and jabbed his finger right in his chest. "You!"

"What about me?" Kevin asked.

"You're responsible for all this!" Alexander said. "You should be arrested!"

"And you should be quiet," Kevin said. "All you did

was rat us out to the aliens who were trying to destroy the world."

"The aliens you brought here!" Alexander whined.

"By accident," Kevin said.

"Speaking of accidents," Warner said. "Take a look at your pants."

Alexander looked down at the pee stain on his leg and frowned.

The whole camp erupted with laughter.

"Three cheers for the Extraordinary Terrestrials!" Little Bobby Little stood in front of the pack and shouted. "Hip hip, hooray!"

"Hip hip, hooray!" everyone but Alexander shouted three times.

Kevin looked around to say good-bye to the Kamilions, but they were nowhere to be seen. "Where'd they go?" Kevin asked. He and Warner, Tara, and TJ looked around. Overhead, the night sky blinked with their cruisers and starships as the Kamilion force soared up out of Earth's atmosphere.

Head Counselor Dimpus walked over to the four of

them and craned his neck up to watch the fleeing aliens. "You kids have some serious explaining to do. . . ."

"Mr. Dimpus, I would love to tell you," Kevin said. "And we totally will, but we kind of sort of have to go save the universe right now."

"But we'll be back as soon as we're done, okay?" said Tara.

"Unless we decide to stay in space and live on an alien planet," Warner said.

"Do we need a permission slip for that?" TJ asked.

Their head counselor seemed a little off-kilter. "Okay, but I'm going to have to notify your parents. . . ."

"Don't worry," Klyk said, walking up behind Dimpus and tapping him on the shoulder. "I'll make sure they get back in one piece."

Dimpus turned around and saw the giant alien cyborg standing before him. The befuddled camp director instantly swooned and fainted to the ground with a thump.

"Is he all right?" Tara asked Klyk.

"Happens sometimes after getting freeze-rayed for too long," Klyk said. "Let him sleep it off."

"You guys think we should call our parents before we go?" TJ said.

"We should probably let them know if we're going all the way to outer space," said Tara.

All things considered, Kevin was pretty sure his parents would let him go save the universe from annihilation if they gave him a chance to explain.

But something told him they weren't going to have time for all that.

ACKNOWLEDGMENTS

I would like to thank Emilia Rhodes for telling me what's what throughout these alien-infested cosmos; to Alice Jerman for not letting the aliens take over my brain; to Sara Shandler and Josh Bank for being kind enough to lend me their telepathy helmets; and to Ryan Harbage for working out the intergalactic peace treaty.

Read a sneak peek of the next adventure!

STARSHIP BLOOPERS

The smell of scorched flesh and alien slime drifted through the night air.

The entire science camp reeked like a bonfire that had just been peed on.

Only a few minutes ago Kevin Brewer and his friends Warner Reed, Tara Swift, TJ Boyd, and an alien cyborg cop named Klyk—had almost been blown up by two of the most dangerous aliens in the galaxy. Zouric and Nuzz were trying to turn the human race into a bunch of robo-slaves. But luckily for the inhabitants of planet Earth, the four friends had used their wormhole generator to blast the evil aliens across the galaxy.

Kevin glanced through the crowd of campers, who were all a bit shell-shocked from the extraterrestrial invasion. Alexander stared back at him with a dirty-diaper scowl on his face. Kevin broke off eye contact with his nemesis and looked over at their head counselor, Mr. Dimpus. The camp director and the other counselors were gathered in a circle, whispering to one another.

For the past eight hours or so, a freeze-ray bomb had immobilized the camp and everyone in it except for Kevin and his friends. The girls' soccer campers from across the lake, as well as an alien race of reptilian warriors, known as Kamilions, had been brainwashed by alien nanobugs designed by Zouric and Nuzz.

It was a lot to process, and Kevin could tell that nobody really knew what was going on. *Probably better that way*, he thought. Kevin wished they had a memory eraser like in the movies, but he'd just have to hope that it would all blow over somehow.

The odds of that happening, he knew, were slim.

In the past twenty-four hours Kevin and his friends had gone from science-camp dorks to interstellar crime fighters who had saved the world not once, but twice in a single day. First thing that morning, before taking down Zouric and Nuzz, they had stopped Mim, a furry purple alien with a mean appetite, from eating their planet.

Kevin couldn't take all the credit, though. If it weren't for a little help from Klyk, their intragalactic bounty hunter friend, the planet would now be brainwashed and their camp would still be frozen in time. They were short a wormhole generator and some force-field gloves. But along with two freeze rays and a shrink ray, there was one other special thing that they had in their possession.

"Let me see that comic book again," Kevin said, and snapped his fingers at TJ.

TJ handed him Max Greyson's latest comic book. The newest edition of the famous comic book series *Brainstorm* had just come through an alien transmitter, materializing as if by magic. Even weirder than that, all the illustrations showed Kevin and his friends taking down Zouric and Nuzz, which had *just* happened. It was almost as if the famous comic book creator had seen the events before they happened.

But that wasn't all Max had sent. His transmission also said he was being held captive in outer space. The entire galaxy, he also said, was in grave danger. Kevin and his friends needed to rescue him before something really bad happened.

What that was, exactly, they had no idea.

They all peered over Kevin's shoulders as he flipped through the comic book. Tara shone a flashlight to see the pages in the dark. "You guys notice anything?"

"Not really, except us being awesome and saving the world!" Warner said.

"The page numbers," Tara gasped. "They're out of order!"

"Maybe that's because they're not page numbers," Kevin said.

"Exactly!" TJ started to write down the digits in a sequence: 2, 3, 5, 13, 89, 233, 1597.

"Do these look familiar?" He showed Kevin, Warner, Tara, and Klyk.

"Two, three, five, and thirteen are all prime

numbers," Kevin said, the wheels turning in his head.

"And eighty-nine, two hundred thirty-three, and fifteen ninety-seven," Tara said. "Those are all primes, too, but they're also part of the Fibonacci sequence. . . ."

Klyk leaned over them as they studied the comic. "Those are coordinates," Klyk told them. "Somewhere

in the Globula Nebula. Near the outer quadrant of the Centaurus arm of the Milky Way."

"Max is telling us where he is!" Warner exclaimed. "I knew he wouldn't leave us hanging like that."

"But that's, like, sixty thousand light years away!" TJ exclaimed. "On the other side of the galaxy."

"Then we better gear up," Warner said, looking through his bag of alien gadgets. "We have two freeze rays and one shrink ray."

"One transmitter," TJ said, and held up the device that had sent the comic book through space and time.

"We should get the telepathy helmet before we go, too," Tara said.

"Who cares about the telepathy helmet?" said Warner. "Let's go find Max Greyson."

"No, she's right," said Klyk. "Telepathy helmets are hard to come by, if not impossible. I have no idea how Mim got one in the first place."

Tara had left the telepathy helmet inside one of the girls' cabins at the soccer camp.

Kevin, Warner, Tara, TJ, and Klyk sprinted off into

the shadowy forest, leaving the rest of the campers and counselors behind. They wove through the trees until they hit the lake. Kevin led the way as they skirted the lake and made their way through the girls' soccer camp.

"Let's go," Klyk said, and pushed the cabin door open with his bionic arm. The kids ducked under and ran inside.

The floorboards creaked as they walked through the empty cabin. Zack's eyes swept back and forth across the floor. The telepathy helmet stuck out from beneath one of the beds.

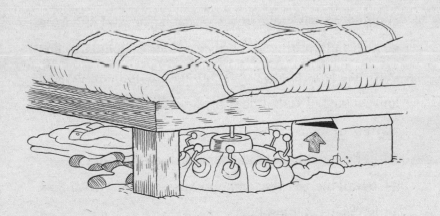

Kevin shuffled across the mattress and hopped off the other side. The high-tech headgear glinted in the moonlight. He bent down and was about to pick up the helmet when a cylinder of magenta light appeared in front of him. The thick beam of light was perfectly round and cast a reddish-purple glow throughout the room.

"What the—" Kevin jumped back, startled. He flinched at the sight in front of him.

An alien had appeared that looked like a giant hairless cat with four eyes across its brow. The feline-esque creature stood on two hind legs and was as big as a tall human, only a few inches shorter than Klyk. Kevin counted six arms total, three on each side, starting from its hips and working up its ribcage to the shoulders. The paws had long, sharp claws coming out of them. It had a long, scaly tail with dinosaur-like spikes that ran all the way up its spine.

The alien looked at them with all four of its eyes as its tail menacingly whapped to and fro. The spikes on its back prickled like a porcupine's as Klyk's hand went slowly for his hip, like a Wild West gunslinger getting ready for a duel.

"Hold it right there!" Klyk said calmly. "Don't move."

But the alien didn't listen. It quickly bent down and snatched up the telepathy helmet in its sixfold clutches.

Klyk drew a small gadget, aimed it at the alien, and fired. Kevin stepped back.

A bolt of electric-blue light zapped across the room and struck the alien in the arm. The beast squawked and disappeared into its magenta beam of light, along with the telepathy helmet held tightly in its paws.

"Did everybody see that?" Tara asked. "'Cause I want to make sure I'm not the only one who just saw a seven-foot, four-eyed cat with six arms and a dinosaur tail. . . ."

"What the heck was that thing?" Kevin asked.

All the kids gazed up at Klyk, who was putting the small remote-control-like gadget back in his hip holster. "That, my friends, was a Sfink. . . ."

"And what's that thing you just shot it with?" TJ asked.

"That was a tracking device," Klyk said. "Give it a minute and it should tell us where he went with our helmet."

"Cool," Warner said. "But what's a Sfink?"

"They're kind of like space pirates," he said. "They're very unfriendly. I've actually never seen one in person. But I've heard stories."

"What kind of space cop are you?" Warner shook his head.

"The galaxy's huge," Klyk said defensively. "I'm more familiar with the aliens in my sector. We've never had a problem with the Sfinks in my neck of the galaxy. Phirf and Drooq would know more about it."

"Who are Phirf and Drooq?" Kevin asked.

"My partners," he said. "The ones *you* zapped with the wormhole generator. They will know more about the Sfinks than I do, since they work in the outer sectors. That's where some of the more unsavory aliens spend their time."

"It doesn't make sense, though," Kevin said. "Why would this alien randomly want our telepathy helmet?"

"I don't think it was random," Tara said.

"But, how did it know that we even had a telepathy helmet?" Kevin said.

"It must have been watching us somehow," TJ suggested.

"Like, it knew exactly where we were," said Warner.

"That's okay, because now we know exactly where

it is . . . check it out." Klyk showed them the readout from the tracking device.

Kevin's eyes bulged with excitement.

The numbers on Klyk's tracker were precisely the same coordinates as the pages of Max Greyson's comic book.

CRAVING ADVENTURE?

Read on for a peek at

John Kloepfer's slimiest series yet.

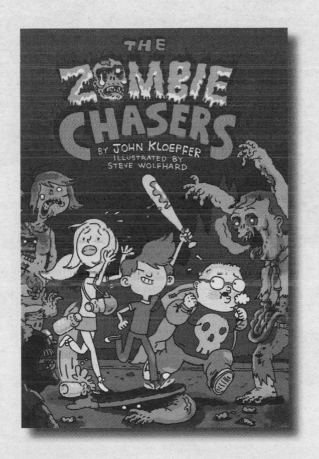

CHAPTER

Dusk settled over the neighborhood. The humid air was thick as pulp.

Zack Clarke turned onto Locust Lane after a slow walk home, expecting the usual Friday night action on his block: the Zimmer twins grinding out tricks on their skateboards across the parkway; Mrs. Mansfield coming home from the video store with bags of fast food and DVDs for her lazy children; or Old Man Stratton prowling the sidewalks, a disintegrating paperback clutched in his veiny hand. But on this muggy Arizona evening, there wasn't a soul to be seen.

Hunched down under the weight of his backpack,

Zack quickened his pace, eager to get home. Earlier in the day, a food fight had landed him in after-school work detention, polishing his middle school's linoleum floors. Now all Zack wanted was the one leftover slice of chocolate birthday cake waiting in the refrigerator, wrapped in plastic and tagged with a Post-it: ZACK'S B-DAY CAKE, DO NOT TOUCH!

Zack could see his house now, his mom's Volvo station wagon sitting in the driveway. Every light in the house was off—all except the one in his sister's bedroom above the garage. He watched from the sidewalk

as Zoe's room went dark, leaving the house looking empty and deserted.

But Zack knew that his older sister, Zoe, and her evil trio of eighth-grade she-devils—Madison Miller, Ryan York, and Samantha Donovan—were having one of their notorious sleepovers at his house. So until Mom and Dad returned from parent-teacher night at his school, it would just be him. And them.

As he reached the stoop, a street lamp flickered and went dead, casting the entire lawn in shadow. He pushed the front door open slowly. "Hello!" he called out into the darkness. "Zoe?"

Suddenly, the door slammed shut, and he felt a paper bag crinkle down over his head. A voice shouted, "Gotcha!"

In an instant, four pairs of hands grabbed Zack by his elbows and ankles, hoisted him off the ground, and began to carry him through the foyer. Caught in their monster-tight grip, Zack squirmed uselessly, unable to twist free.

His captors plopped him down hard on an old

wooden desk chair, the bag still over his head. Someone was holding his wrists behind the chair, bending his arms back as if he were a handcuffed prisoner. He writhed and kicked, trying to buck loose. Frustrated and exhausted, Zack went limp, playing possum for a second, before thrashing wildly in one final burst of energy.

That's when he heard a digital beep, and someone lifted the bag off his head. His sister, Zoe, stood before him. Directly behind her, their father's laptop sat open on the coffee table, and Zack could see himself on the computer screen.

"Zoe, what are you doing? You know Dad doesn't let us play with the webcam."

"I'm not playing, little brother," she said, flipping her dark hair back and cocking her head all too glamorously, like America's Next Top Psycho preparing for her closeup. "I'm producing a new reality show for VH1. It's called *Hostage Makeover*. You want to be in it?" A sinister grin stretched across her face.

"I'd rather die in my own vomit," Zack answered.

"Tough luck, kiddo," Zoe snickered. "Look alive, girls!"

Samantha and Ryan entered the living room and shimmied behind Zack. Ryan held a giant roll of duct tape in one hand, and when Zack turned around, she tucked it behind her back. "No peeking, young Zachariah!" she chided, patting him on the head.

"Okay, Zacky, you hold still!" Zoe gestured to her two minions. A second later, Ryan and Samantha were circling Zack, taping his upper arms and shoulders firmly to the back of the chair, quickly moving on to his legs until they were sure he couldn't escape. The

mysterious pair of hands behind him finally unclasped his wrists. Zack felt the blood rush, throbbing in his fingertips.

Again, he tried to wriggle free, but the tape was too strong.

Zoe adjusted the webcam to capture her brother's struggle. Then she crouched down in front of the computer and spoke: "Welcome to the premiere of *Hostage Makeover*. I am your host, Zoe Clarke. You've already met our captive, my unfortunate-looking younger brother, Zachary Arbutus Clarke." She stepped away from the laptop. "Tell us how you're feeling, Hostage Boy."

"Zoe, seriously, lay off." Zack said.

"Zoe, seriously, lay off," a voice mimicked him.

Madison Miller emerged from behind the chair, holding a polka-dotted makeup case. Madison was the prettiest girl in school, with long, almost blond, light brown hair, and just a few faint freckles dotting her button nose. She was also one of the tallest girls in the eighth grade, and she towered over Zack, gazing down at him with her big blue eyes.

"Shut up, Madison. No one's talking to you."

"Shut up, Madison. No one's talking to you," Madison continued in her baby voice.

"Stop copying me," Zack insisted.

"Stop copying me." Madison wouldn't quit.

"I'm an idiot," Zack said, trying to outsmart her.

"Yes, Zachary, I'm afraid you are."

Game over.

Madison opened up the makeup case and pulled out what looked like colored pencils. Then she took a sip of her favorite drink, kiwi-strawberry VitalVeganPowerPunch.

"You know, Madison," Zack said. "I heard something, that if you drink too much of that

stuff it can, like, mess with your whole biological makeup."

"Did someone say 'makeup'?" Zoe chirped.

With that, Madison pulled out a frightening array of cosmetics and placed them on the coffee table. Zack had no idea what all this stuff was used for, other than cluttering up Zoe's bathroom.

"Listen up, little bro." Zoe formed a little rectangle with her index fingers and thumbs and peered through it like some kind of Hollywood director. "If you play nice, we're gonna make you look really, really pretty. But if you disturb me while I'm filming, we will make you look silly, then I will lock you in your room, put this video on YouTube, and email the link to everyone at school. Now be a good hostage."

"Zoe, let me go or I'll tell Mom and Dad that you've been sneaking out of the house at night," Zack blurted in desperation.

"Oh, dear brother," Zoe sneered. "Good hostages don't make threats."

She hit the space bar and yelled, "Action!"

BLAST OFF WITH GALAXY'S MOST WANTED

BOOK 1

BOOK 2

BOOK 3